A NEW BEGINNING

KATIE MONGELLI

Monarch Dreams Publishing, LLC

For Alexis,
Don't ever put your dreams up on a shelf, but if you do, it is never too late to dust them off.

xo

Chapter 1

Catherine rests her palms on the edge of the bathroom sink and closes her eyes, taking in a deep breath.

"You're lucky to be alive."

The doctor's cruel words echo in her mind.

Cursed would be more accurate, she thinks to herself as she hears the bathroom door swing open and a gaggle of giggling interns enter, their high heels clicking on the tile floor. Her spine tenses and she grabs a paper towel and dabs the tears away from the corner of her eyes, careful not to smudge her make-up. She checks her reflection in the mirror, tucking a loose strand of wavy brown hair behind one ear and adds a touch of lipstick. A sigh floats out of her lips before she can hold it back. *No time for this pity party now*, she thinks, smoothing her suit skirt. She ducks out of the bathroom, trying to avoid the sight of the boisterous 20-something girls.

Her client Jim is waiting for her in the lobby of Vertus Technologies. She squares her shoulders and puts on her best smile.

"So good to see you," he says as he scoops her into a

warm hug. "Let's go meet in my office. Julie, can you bring us some coffee please?" Jim puts his arm around her shoulder, and leads her down a long hallway, passing offices full of junior executives absorbed in their laptops, and says good morning to each employee along the way.

They enter the office and Jim points towards the two chairs next to his desk. "Have a seat."

Catherine sits down, taking in the family photos displayed behind his desk and asks, "How's your family doing?"

Jim leans back in his chair clasping his hands behind his head. His face lights up. "Cassie called last night telling us she got the Little Bunny award in her kindergarten class. Apparently, she has mastered tying her shoes!" Jim laughs proudly at his granddaughter's accomplishment.

Catherine smiles warmly and opens her briefcase, "I have prepared an agenda and attached the quarterly financials for your review," she says handing Jim the packet of papers.

Jim sits up straighter, takes a long sip of his coffee and sets the mug back down on the desk before beginning, "I didn't call you here to review the financials." He rubs his chin, then stands and walks over to the bookshelf, picking up a framed photo of his kids and grandkids at the beach, suntanned and smiling. "This was all just a dream when we started working together, wasn't it?"

Catherine nods her agreement. Jim was her first client when he started Vertus Technologies the same week she started her CPA firm.

"I guess that old saying is true, time flies when you are having fun," she says, wishing he would stop the trip down memory lane and get to his point.

"That's what I am worried about." He sits down, leaning forward resting his hands on his knees and says, "we have worked together for over 20 years and I have never seen you like this."

Catherine fidgets in her seat as Jim continues, "I would be lying if I said I understood how painful it was for you losing Aleksandra, but it's been over a year and I'm worried about you."

Catherine tries to put on a smile and say something reassuring, but she just sits there silently staring down at her "but first coffee" mug.

Jim runs his fingers through his thinning gray hair before folding his arms across his chest. "You aren't taking care of yourself and I care about you too much to sit back and watch this. I'm sorry, I have to do this, for you."

Catherine shifts in her chair, "I don't think I understand. What are you doing for me?" she asks.

"I am taking you off my account. Your team can keep working on the financials, but we are taking a break."

"You're firing me?"

Jim gently put his hand on her shoulder, "It's just a break, trust me, you need this."

Catherine picks up her briefcase and pauses before opening the door. "I don't think you have any idea what I need right now."

"I may not have lost my daughter, but I have lived a lot of years. Work isn't what you need right now."

She rushes down the hallway and smacks the elevator button repeatedly before heading for the stairs. Rummaging through her purse, she takes the stairs two at a time. She pulls out her cell phone dialing Nelly, but the connection fails. Exiting the building, she climbs in her car and lets the tears fall. She feels her phone buzzing with an incoming call and sees from the display that it's Nelly.

"Hey Sweetie, how does your day look?" Nelly asks.

"Don't ask!" Catherine replies.

"Do you want to talk about it over lunch?"

"I can't. How about coffee?"

"On my way! See you soon!"

The scent of freshly roasted coffee beans waft out the door of The Daily Grind coffee shop as Catherine walks in. She hears the quiet hum of espresso machines and the indie music that is distinct to coffee shops

"Excuse me," Catherine says, noticing the man behind the counter in a t-shirt that shows off just enough of his biceps that you could see it flex as he cleaned off his hands on a towel.

"Hey there," he responds, turning and offering a warm smile.

Catherine stutters, lost in his green eyes framed by fine lines that tell of years of smiles and sadness. "Umm, I would like a green tea, a pumpkin spice latte, and a chocolate croissant."

He lets out a hearty laugh. "I am not going to be able to help you with that."

Catherine looks around the shop and sees other customers enjoying their drinks. "Is the espresso machine broken?"

"I think the machines are doing just fine," he shrugs.

"Don't mind Blake!" says a bubbly and petite girl with a name tag that reads Leenie. "He's just giving you a hard time. I don't know how he can be a genius at fixing the bakery case but a complete knucklehead when it comes to making espresso." She elbows him while taking Catherine's order.

"You let me stand there and make a fool of myself? You could have at least told me you didn't work here."

"And ruin all the fun you were having?" He laughs again.

"Make yourself comfortable and I'll bring these over to you when they are ready," Leenie says.

Catherine finds a quiet table near the stone fireplace and opens her laptop to read through emails before Nelly arrives.

"Who's the cute new guy behind the counter?" Nelly says, greeting Catherine with a hug before sitting down. "I will take an order of that to go," she laughs.

Catherine rolls her eyes. "He may look yummy, but he's a real smart ass."

"Here we go ladies. Can I get you anything else?" Blake says, setting their drinks down.

"That's so sweet! How have I not seen you in here before?" Nelly asks.

"Just helping out for the day," he says and winks at Catherine. Then he heads back to making repairs on the bakery case.

"He seemed nothing but sweet to me," Nelly says, "and I think he is into you!"

"You know how I feel about dating."

"Come on, you haven't been in a relationship in years. He is definitely checking you out," Nelly says, glancing back to the counter.

"There's a reason I've been single all these years. Guys are all the same. Once they know they have you hooked, they leave you. Besides, I am doing just fine on my own."

"Then why are you still checking him out?"

"Shush! Anyway, how are the kids?"

"The kids are kids, they are fine. What are you working on?"

Catherine sighs. "Jim thinks I need to take some time

off and I have no idea what to do. I feel like staying busy is what I need right now."

"Oh, sweetheart, I'm sorry." Nelly reaches over and takes Catherine's hands in hers. "Why don't you go out to your lake house?"

"It's on the market and I don't want to interfere with any showings the real estate agent may have planned."

"I still can't believe you are selling it. You love that house!"

"Correction. I loved that house, but now, it's not the same."

"I think Jim is right. Some rest would do you some good," Nelly explains, lovingly rubbing Catherine's arm.

"When I talked to the agent, he said if I am serious about selling it then I need to renovate. 'Buyers want updated kitchens and bathrooms!'" Catherine says, mimicking her agent's suggestion.

"That's perfect," Nelly squeals.

"What would be perfect?"

"You should go to the lake house and get the renovations done!"

"My agent said if I hire someone soon it could be done before New Year's."

"You love the peace and quiet of being near the water, and soon, it will snow. This could be so good for you."

"I just want to get the renovations done, so it is a quick sale and I can get back to here, to my work."

Nelly continues, "You know, we are all just worried about you because we love you."

"I'm fine," Catherine says, unconsciously tinkering with the horseshoe necklace around her neck.

Nelly gently puts her hand on Catherine's arm. "You won't even mention her name. You won't talk to me or your doctor. You aren't sleeping. It's been over a year. You can't keep going on like this! It's time you live again, she would want that for you!" Nelly pleads with her.

"I'll think about it."

Nelly grins.

Catherine feels her phone buzzing. "It's my office, I have to get this and get going to my meeting."

Catherine offers a small wave toward the counter. As she heads out the door she pauses, "I didn't get your name?"

"It's Blake," he says, coming out from behind the counter to shake her hand.

Catherine smiles and reaches for his hand, tripping over his toolbox and dropping her phone.

Blake picks up her phone. "I was just teasing you earlier," he says, handing it back to her, but he doesn't let go. "You should smile more; it looks good on you," he laughs.

Catherine blushes and mumbles, "I have to go" and heads for the door.

Blake calls after her, "forgetting something?"

Catherine, feeling the heat rising to her face, accepts the phone from his outstretched hand and joins him laughing.

Chapter 2

That night, she tosses and turns in bed a few times before letting out a heavy sigh and throwing back the covers. She sits up, rubs the sleep out of her eyes and checks the bedside clock. 3:45 AM. Sighing again she shuffles over to her closet feeling for the light switch and instead bumps into the doorway. After turning on the light, she squints and reaches around on her shelf to find her favorite leggings and sweatshirt and slides them on. She brews a cup of coffee and looks around her house. No job, no Aleksandra, no purpose. *What am I doing here?* She thinks to herself.

She sends a text to Nelly, "I feel trapped in this house and I need to get away. Going to the lake. Will call you later. XO." She gets in the car to make the two-hour drive.

As the sun rises, she takes in the outline of the rolling hills covered in tall grasses, goldenrod, and soft brown velvet topped cattails. The leaves have fallen, and the trees are bare. She can see the silhouette of a farm sitting atop the hill and a creek cutting through the center of the property with a small bridge connecting the pastures. She imagines what it will be like to pass the morning on the porch swing of the farm house, taking in the smell of the pines at the end of the fields, while eating a slice of freshly baked apple pie made from the trees in the yard.

She approaches a sharp curve in the road and pulls over onto the shoulder. She feels a chill as she steps out of the car and pulls her coat close to protect herself from the mountain air.

Running her hand along the still mangled guard rail, she picks up a dirty matted stuffed dog from the makeshift memorial and hugs it close. She crawls over the guardrail and makes her way down the embankment. At the bottom of the hill the creek is flowing and she recalls the cold water beneath her body and the oddly peaceful feeling of her hair floating on the water while the soft rain hit her face. She recalls how tears streamed down her cheeks as she listened, unable to move, as Aleksandra cried like a scared infant in the middle of the night, "Mama! Mama!"

In the hospital the doctor told her, she was lucky to be alive and relayed the details of the crash to her. He told her how the old man had crossed into her lane and she swerved, avoiding the crash. The old man saw her car go down the embankment, called 911, and then he climbed down the wet rocky slope where the car was resting upside down. He found Aleksandra and held her hand and stroked her hair until the ambulance arrived. He was there for her when she couldn't be. *I am so thankful to him that she wasn't alone*, Catherine thinks, *but I know she needed me and I wasn't there for her.*

She collapses to her knees in the blanket of leaves and cries, "Why did you take her from me?"

She sobs and longs to hold her daughter in her arms just one more time, brush the hair off her face and kiss her forehead. *There were so many things I didn't get to tell you. How am I supposed to go on without you?* She wonders.

She feels her phone vibrating in her jacket pocket and knows Nelly is checking on her. How could she tell Nelly that she is racing to the lake house in the early morning hours chasing the warmth she had with Aleksandra? How could she possibly explain that she feels Aleksandra calling her to the lake house?

Everyone says I have to accept this new life, she thinks, *but I just feel broken. How can they expect me to move on? They told me the sadness and loneliness would fade. They told me the worst was over, but now, a year later, it feels as painful as that first night. What do they know?*

She pulls the car into the driveway of the lake house and sees the last of the fog burning off the lake as the sun rises higher into the sky. Catherine walks to the front door of the house, pulling the key out of the secret place in the frog's mouth, but pauses before turning the knob. She hasn't been inside the lake house in over a year.

"Why did you bring me back here? I'm not ready for this," she whispers to Aleksandra. She takes a deep breath, her hand shaking, and opens the door. Inside the mudroom, everything is just as she remembers it. She feels like she is coming back home after a weekend away. Her eyes immediately dart to Aleksandra's muddy riding boots sitting on the shoe tray inside the door. Catherine picks them up and hugs them close as she walks into the family room.

She opens the living room curtains to let in the morning sun, sneezing as the dust floats free. The beams of sunlight coming in through the window highlight the traffic pattern worn in the carpet from years of bare feet.

She follows that path to the white linoleum in the kitchen and opens the freezer, bare except for the tin of ground coffee she pulls out to brew. While the coffee percolates, she opens the cabinet and pulls out a mug and leans back against the counter. She stares across at the empty sink, where dirty dishes used to pile up like a mountain, waiting to be washed.

Coffee in hand, she walks out the back door onto the deck. The echo of the birds squawking signals the change of seasons as they migrate south for winter. She heads down the stairs and follows the gravel path down to the dock. The water in the lake is low before the winter ahead, and shimmering bits of white sea-glass dot the shoreline. Catherine picks up a piece feeling its jagged edge and drops it. *This rock isn't ready,* she thinks. Another season or two of water pounding over it will soften its rough edges.

Sitting on the dock and closing her eyes she listens to the gentle lapping of the water as it hits the shore and inhales the scent of the fresh air. She reaches down feeling the water, icy cold as the cooler winter weather moves in. The first time she and Aleksandra sat in this spot together, she was nine months pregnant, anxiously awaiting the arrival of her little one. The doctor said she shouldn't be traveling to the lake and should stay close to home because she could go into labor any day, but she didn't care. The town had its own hospital and she would be fine.

She had been traveling to the lake for weekend getaways since she was a small girl. It had always been her favorite place to relax and play. As her business grew, so did her desire to have a place at the lake and with her baby on the way she was combing the listings, looking to make her dream part of their future. Browsing through the listings she paused at one she recognized. She had seen this house for years and always loved it more than any others.

She picked up the phone and asked to see it right away before someone else made it theirs. She drove up to the lake that day and made an offer. The owners accepted it immediately and she went down to the dock to celebrate. She remembers rubbing her belly and talking to her baby about all the memories they were going to make here. She told her how they were going to swim in the lake on hot summer days and play in the snow in the winter. She talked of the adventures they would share.

"It's you and me forever," she said. That day, she already knew her little one and couldn't imagine how much their love would grow.

As Aleksandra got older they would dip their toes into the water and watch the water dance through the rocks. They would talk all evening watching the sun slowly drop below the horizon. Something about this spot was simply magical. It was as if the water was a cure for all that ailed them.

Catherine gets up and walks over to the patio where two Adirondack chairs sit next to the fire pit. She isn't sure how long she sits like this, but she feels more peaceful than she has felt in ages.

Chapter 3

Catherine sits up in bed and rubs her eyes, when she hears the doorbell ringing. Startled, she hops out of bed and throws on a sweatshirt she finds laying on the end of the bed and pulls her hair up into a messy bun with an elastic from her wrist. On the way down the stairs she wipes the sleep from the corner of her eyes and heads into the mudroom to open the door.

"Coffee guy?" She says looking down realizing she is in her pajamas. "What? What are you doing here?"

"Good morning. Thanks for answering the door."

"Sorry, were you waiting?"

"A little while."

"Why? What are you doing here in Pine Lake??"

"I've been hired to do the renovations on this house. What are you doing here?"

"You're my contractor?" Catherine asks.

"Guilty as charged," Blake says, kicking the dirt of his boots. "Can I come in or are you going to leave me out here to freeze?"

"Oh, sorry, yes come in," Catherine says, stepping back

out the doorway to let Blake in the mudroom.

"Did I wake you?" Blake asks.

Catherine's face flushes and she awkwardly crosses her arms across her chest, hoping he doesn't notice she isn't wearing a bra.

"I need just a minute," she says, leading him down the hallway into the kitchen. "Make yourself comfortable and I will be right back." She eases out of the kitchen and races back upstairs to change.

She tears open her overnight bag searching for some jeans and a top and fumbles, tripping over the pant legs trying to get them on and falls down.

"Is everything ok up there?" Blake calls out.

"Fine, I'm fine! I'll be down in just a minute," she spits through toothpaste while desperately brushing. Then she fixes her ponytail and applies a dab of lip gloss before heading back down to the kitchen.

"I'm sorry, I never oversleep. I don't know what happened."

"This mountain air does that to a person."

"What were you doing in the city the other day?" She asks, opening the freezer and grabbing out the tin of coffee.

"My niece, Leenie, owns The Daily Grind. I help her out with repairs now and again."

"But you live out here?"

"Uh-huh," Blake responds, accepting the mug of black coffee. "No fancy pumpkin spice lattes today?"

"Ha-ha, I see you were paying attention," Catherine says, pouring herself a fresh mug of coffee and joining Blake at the kitchen table.

"I don't just go around delivering coffee to all the customers. I have standards," Blake says, setting down his coffee mug.

"Tell me, how long have you had your place?" turning in his seat to look around.

Catherine leans forward, resting her elbows on the table holding her coffee mug in both hands, "I bought it about 17 years ago."

"Your real estate agent, Rich, called me yesterday."

"Have you worked together before?" Catherine asks.

"All the time. His son, Drew, and I have been best friends since we could walk. And, I'm the best in town."

Catherine nods her head, listening.

"He said something about you needing the renovations done quickly."

"I want to list it for sale by New Year's, but Rich said I need to do a lot of updates, if I want any solid offers."

"It's a great place, but I agree. Why are you selling?" Blake asks.

"Things change. It's time for a fresh start."

"I don't think I could let go of a place like this."

They both sit in silence, awkwardly staring into their coffee, unsure of what to say next.

Catherine looks up and breaks the silence "Would you like a tour and you can tell me your ideas?"

"That sounds like a good plan."

She leads the way into the living room. "Rich says the buyers want modern kitchens and bathrooms, but I want it to have a rustic feel."

"How rustic are we talking?" Blake asks, walking around the room taking it in.

"I don't want a hunting lodge, so high end finishes and elegance, but with some charm. Maybe some wood beams in the ceiling here and reclaimed wood floors throughout?"

"This space has great potential," Blake says, opening the fireplace and inspecting it.

"That was our favorite part of this room," Catherine says, indicating the fireplace.

"Our? I didn't realize you were married," Blake says looking sheepish.

Catherine laughs. "Me, married? Hell no!" But then she drops her gaze towards her feet. "My daughter. We spent a lot of winter nights…" She pauses.

"Well, it really is a great feature, and I think we should keep it as is. We could open up the wall to the kitchen where we could add an oversized island. It will be great for entertaining," Blake says.

Catherine nods silently, a little disconcerted by his repetitive us of the word "we."

"Shall we head in here next?" Blake says reaching for the door right off the living room.

She steps in front of the door. "No, that room doesn't need any work."

"Why don't I just make sure? Once we open these walls and put in new flooring we may need to make changes here, too, so it all flows."

"No. It stays as it is," she says.

He takes his hand off the door knob, shakes his head and crosses his arms across his chest thinking for a minute and then says, "My name is on this project and I don't want to risk my reputation with sloppy work. I think I should check it out."

"Like I said, it stays as it is."

Blake throws up his hands in surrender. "As you wish," he says mockingly.

Catherine walks him to the mudroom.

"I will get these notes drawn up and we can start right away. I know it can be stressful, but trust me, you're going to love it. You may not even want to sell it when I'm done."

"Don't worry, I will be selling it."

"Ok, I'll be back this weekend to hang some plastic sheeting. You won't have a working kitchen for a while, but it doesn't look like you eat much so I think we'll be ok," Blake laughs.

"What do you mean?" Catherine asks.

"I meant that you look skinny. Did I say something wrong? I thought women liked being called skinny?"

"This sort of sounds sexist."

Blake nods, "Sorry, I meant it in a good way."

"Okay," Catherine says mostly to herself, blushing as she closes the door. She leans against the door smiling and enjoying the rare feeling of the butterflies in her stomach.

With new eyes she pours a fresh cup of coffee and wanders into the living room. Picking up her cell phone she sees a text from Nelly and dials her number. Nelly picks up on the first ring.

"How does it feel being back?" she asks.

"It's quiet. Too quiet," Catherine says, sitting on the sofa, stretching her legs out, leaning back on the sofa cushions.

"You haven't slowed down in years, maybe a little quiet will do you good."

"Maybe," Catherine stares out at the lake considering Nelly's idea. "I had 16 years of laughter, sleepovers, and impromptu dance parties. What am I supposed to do now?"

"If I had a quiet day I would take a nap. Maybe you could start there?"

Catherine sets her coffee down on the table and walks over to the built in's where she has pictures of them displayed. "It doesn't matter what I do, I can't have what I want."

"You haven't tried this yet! Just give it a chance. Maybe you can have what you want."

Chapter 4

The next morning, Catherine wanders through the house taking a final look at their place before it is dismantled. Suddenly it becomes obvious how badly she needs to get out of there. She jumps in her car and drives to the "Shops on the Water" along main street Pine Lake.

After parking she follows the cobbled path along the boutiques and restaurants. As she passes the Lakeside Boutique and sees her reflection in the shop window, she turns to examine her profile. She remembers Blake's comment from the day before.

I am vanishing, she thinks, noticing how her clothes hang on her frame like a wire hanger. *What is happening to me?* She picks up her pace until she reaches the community center and yanks the door open. At the front desk she searches the depths of her purse for her membership card.

"It's okay if you don't have your card, Ma'am. We can just look you up by name," the kid behind the front desk informs her.

"Yeah, I can't seem to find it, so that would be great."

"No worries, Ma'am. You're all checked in. Here is the

group fitness class schedule and cardio fit starts in five minutes in studio one."

Catherine looks down at what she is wearing.

"This won't work for the Cardio fit class!" a fit and bubbly red headed woman states.

"Maybe this whole idea was a mistake," Catherine says, heading for the front door.

"Yes, you're right, this outfit was a mistake. Let's get you fixed up," the red headed woman says, leading Catherine to the gym's athletic store. She sizes Catherine up and pulls a sports bra and tank top from the racks and shoves Catherine into a changing room. "Put these on and then we will get you a bottle of water from the café."

Catherine just nods agreement and changes as directed. She pulls on the Lycra workout pants noticing how her once curvy and feminine hips look more square and bony and her athletic and muscular legs barely demand the extra small sized pants to stretch as she slips them on. She turns in the mirror taking herself in from all angles.

"Hurry up, we need to get in there before all the places up front are taken."

"I'm not sure this is a good idea," Catherine says from the changing room.

"Trust me, your ass will thank me later," the red head says, dragging Catherine down the hallway to the aerobics studio and up to the front and center of fitness studio. "By the way, I'm Ginger," she says, smiling.

A lean and fit instructor comes in wearing a headset and turns on some loud fast paced pop music. The fitness instructor speaks into her microphone. "Who's ready to move?"

The women in the class begin to clap and march in place following the lead of the instructor who picks up the pace. "Who's with me, let's do this. 3-2-1," she prods and starts moving side to side and adding in some pumping arm movements.

Catherine stumbles to keep up with the direction and speed of the moves. She looks over to Ginger for guidance. Ginger has the routine mastered and is adding her own twist to the well-choreographed aerobic dance routine. Feeling lost, Catherine heads over to the water fountain for a break with a plan to sneak out the back.

Ginger comes over to get her, "Don't give up now!" She links arms with Catherine, leading her back to their spots at the front of the class. "You'll pick it up!"

What was I thinking, trying this class? Catherine wonders to herself.

The instructor continues barking out commands as she changes directions and adds in more kicks and turns. "Show me you mean business! You have to earn that body! Give me one more!"

Catherine is out of breath as she calls out to Ginger, "is this over yet?"

"No, that was the first circuit. The second one is crazier than the first. You will wonder how she ever dreamt it up!"

"Great. I can't wait," Catherine says, rolling her eyes.

"All right ladies, let's put on our ankle weights and turn up the heat. The next round is double time. Let's pick up the pace. Feel that burn!" the instructor calls out.

Catherine's face is red, sweat dripping from her face as she tries to keep up in the final rounds.

Finally the instructor leads them into stretching and cool down. "That's it, ladies! See you back here next week!"

Catherine picks up one of the gym towels from the back of the room and dabs at the sweat dripping down her face. "That was the craziest workout I have ever done."

Ginger puts her arm around her shoulder "I was completely shocked after my first class with her, but it is such a good workout that I come back to her class whenever I am in town."

"You're not from around here?"

"No way! I tried it once, but I need my big city life."

"Is there anywhere nearby for a smoothie?" Catherine asks.

"Now I know why you are so skinny. Come with me, I know just the place!"

They exit the community center and walk back along the path. The row of shops looks out on the lake. The docks sit empty and the water is as smooth as glass. You can see the outline of the pine trees in its reflection.

The fresh pine wreath at the entrance of the café announces "Season's Greetings" in red calligraphy. Inside the café, there is a stone fireplace with a roaring fire in the corner surrounded by overstuffed chairs arranged in small groups. The café smells of coffee and freshly baked pumpkin pie. Carrying their hot chocolates topped with whip cream and generous slices of pie, they sit down in the corner near the fire, close enough to the Christmas tree that they can smell the scent of fresh pine. The chubby Christmas tree is cheerily decorated with colorful bulbs that reflect the twinkle lights, and touches of silver tinsel hang from the ends of the pine branches.

"I'm telling you this is the best pie in the whole damn country," Ginger declares.

"I can't eat all this."

"Live a little. You just worked out. Me, I just look at a pie and gain five pounds. How do you stay so tiny?"

"You come out here often?" Catherine asks, taking a big bite of her pie.

"One of my best girlfriends lives out here, so I come to visit her occasionally. What about you?"

"I am taking a sabbatical from work."

"This weekend I was feeling a little emotional. I just decided to go through with my divorce, you know how that is."

"Not really, I never married, but I have seen how painful it can be."

"I guess the marriage was over before it started."

"I'm sure, it is still sad."

"I'm ok with that part. Realizing I am giving up my dream to be a mother is what is breaking my heart."

"What do you mean?"

Ginger stirs her coffee in silence, lost in her own thoughts.

Letting out a sigh, "Tick Tock Tick Tock. A single woman at my age doesn't have much time, if you know what I mean," Ginger says.

Catherine puts her hand gently on Ginger's, "You know, there are plenty of divorced women who go on to be moms."

"I'm not following you," Ginger says.

"Well, for starters you could adopt or do IVF."

"I guess I always thought of those as options for couples struggling to have a baby, not a single woman."

"That's how I had my daughter."

"You had your daughter on your own?" Ginger asks surprised.

"I knew I wanted to be a mom, but marriage wasn't for me."

"That's so brave. I don't think I could do it on my own."

"Who's to say you have to do it alone. With your looks and personality, you could have any man you wanted."

"You would think so, but men date me because I'm good arm candy for whatever important gala they have to attend that weekend. They don't see me as the type of woman who will raise the next senator for their family."

Catherine nods sympathetically. "I know what it feels like to want something you can't have. The right man will appreciate all that you have to offer."

"You have been such a good listener, thank you."

"I didn't realize how late it has gotten, I need to get going," Catherine says.

"I'm going to be back in town next weekend. We should have a girl's day and get a mani-pedi. I know the perfect salon and will make appointments for us," Ginger squeals and hugs Catherine goodbye.

As she slides into her car she gives one last wave to Ginger and wonders if she was brave to do things on her own all those years.

Chapter 5

On the drive back home, Catherine decides to go for a walk at Falls Park. She has never seen the redwood forest, but imagines this is what it is like each time she pulls into the park, staring in awe of the dense trees on either side of the drive. Both sides of the lane are surrounded by old growth, thick with eastern hemlock and white pine trees. The trees form a dense canopy of shade so that there is only moss and hearty ferns crawling along the forest floor. She parks the car and heads down the path towards the falls. The damp earth and moss absorb all the sounds creating stillness and silence. She can't think of a single weekend they came to the lake and didn't visit the falls.

After so many years she knows every twist and turn of the path, and quietly meanders through the forest noticing the rocks and the ferns and the fungi growing on the sides of the trees. On the ground she sees two acorns connected like twins and picks them up. She has always collected little treasures she finds and displays them around her house to remind her of the peace she finds on her quiet walks. A young deer pops through the trees and looks at her before dashing back into the forest right before her favorite rock outcropping.

She puts her blanket down on the rocks and lies on her back clasping her hands behind her head. With her eyes closed, she feels the sun on her face and listens to the sounds of the water flowing through the rocks. She remembers that their last visit to Falls Park was shortly before homecoming.

Aleksandra had been excited because the boy she had a huge crush on, Jackson, had asked her as his date. He was all she talked about all day long and Catherine could only hope, Jackson felt the same way about her!

They visited Lakeside Boutique in town to shop for the perfect homecoming dress. The shop was stocked and had long dresses and short dresses and lace dresses with the perfect shoes and accessories to finish any homecoming look. The dressing room was laid out like any girl's fantasy, with a platform on one end surrounded by mirrors and a comfortable sofa for moms to watch their daughters model each look.

After what felt like a hundred dresses Aleksandra picked a short teal flowy dress with a high neckline and lace up detailing in the back. It was simple but striking with her alabaster skin and strawberry blonde hair. She paired it with a strappy pair of silver sandals and small dangle earrings. Catherine was rendered speechless at Aleksandra's transformation from her young daughter in jeans and a sweater into a beautiful young woman headed off to a dance. She caught her breath and gasped, "it is gorgeous!" They both knew this was the look for the dance and headed to the counter to check out and celebrate their shopping success, as they always did, with a picnic lunch at Falls Park.

Catherine tears up at the memory and thinks *Is this the*

new me? Can I just go one day at a time without fighting back the tears?

She gives up on trying to fight them and just allows them to come. In a loud heave she lets out a sob and the tears stream down her cheeks and fall off her chin into her lap. She would give anything to have one more afternoon with her daughter. She promises she would listen to every little teenage drama with rapt attention if she could just go back and do it over. She will have the enthusiasm for a 16-year-old excited for her first dance with a boy she likes, hoping the night will end with the romantic first kiss that she has been fanaticizing about for years. Instead she is sitting in their spot, alone. As she catches her breath, she wipes her face on the sleeve of her sweater and opens up her bag and pulls her pen and journal out and begins to write.

Dear Aleksandra,

I heard you in my dream calling me here, but I am not sure why. I thought I would arrive here and it would be so clear. I thought I would step back into the lake house and feel connected to you. I sat down on the dock like we used to do and waited for you. I don't know what exactly I expected. I came here to Falls Park today thinking that if I visited one of our old favorite places you would call to me.

It's been a year since I've been here. I don't understand what I am supposed to do here. What is it that you want me to see? Where do you want me to go? I feel lost and confused! Tell me why you wanted me to come here! I am.....

She hears the sound of feet approaching and closes her journal and looks around to see Blake and two yellow dogs.

Blake walks over to where she's sitting and crouches

down next to her. "A little cold to be out here visiting the falls today, don't you think?"

Closing her journal, Catherine replies "I guess I could say the same to you. Who are these girls?"

Sitting down next to her, Blake pats the yellow labs on their heads and scratches their necks. "This is Mason and this is Annie." Blake takes off their leashes and gives them a little pat, "go play."

One of the labs runs off back towards the woods, sniffing and playing, and the other curls up and puts her head in Catherine's lap and looks up at her. She pets the dog, "You're such a cutie."

"That's Annie. She's a real love bug. What were you working on?" Blake asks.

"It is just my journal," she says, placing it back into her backpack and zipping it closed.

"You seemed in deep thought, creating big ideas?"

"I love this spot. The tourists all gather around the waterfall and take pictures, but it is quieter here. I can hear myself think."

Blake looks around, taking in the mountain laurel lining the bank across the river, and the hills covered in pines rising to meet the blue sky. "It's my favorite spot in the park, too."

"I think she likes you," Blake says, looking at Annie sleeping against Catherine's lap. "These girls just love the fresh air," Blake says, patting his two yellow Labradors on the neck.

"It's getting late. I think I should head back home," Catherine says.

"Me too. I will walk back with you." He stands and offers her his hand to help her up. They fold her blanket together before heading back onto the trail.

They start their walk along the rocky path, each lost in

their own thoughts, enjoying the feeling of the breeze on their faces and the sound of the leaves rustling in the wind.

Catherine sees a triple acorn in the path and stops to pick it up.

"Isn't this amazing?" she asks, showing Blake the acorns.

"Are you saving acorns?" Blake asks with a smirk.

"How often do you find a perfect set of three acorns all attached? Isn't it magical?"

"I guess."

Undeterred by his lack of enthusiasm, she is even more passionate in trying to convince him how miraculous nature is.

"Nature is so amazing. Just think this tiny little acorn could one day grow to be as tall as these old trees."

Catherine takes another look at her acorn and carefully tucks it into her sweater pocket.

Blake watches her and smiles, then looks up taking in the tops of the trees around them.

"How is that acorn going to grow into one of these trees, if it is in your pocket?"

Catherine laughs.

Blake turns towards Catherine and asks, "You never told me, why are you selling your lake house?"

"I guess I just don't get up here much anymore."

Blake nods in understanding and they continue their walk along the trail.

"It's a shame, you know."

"Why's that?"

"When the real estate market boomed a few years back, developers bought up and divided the last of the large open lots on the lake. There aren't any large water-front properties like yours left. I can't imagine I would ever want to be anywhere else if I had your place."

She smiles and nods. Aleksandra had expressed that exact same sentiment at least a million times whenever they needed to head home, back to their real life.

"Have you lived anywhere else?"

"No. Basically, I've lived here my whole life. For a little while, I planned to head to the coast of North Carolina and study, but I stayed. I tried the city for a bit too, but it wasn't my style. I guess this is home to me. I can't live without the fresh air, the trees, the snow, the water!"

"Yeah, I can see that. With work, being in the city is best for me."

Blake reaches into his bag and pulls out some trail mix. He opens the trail mix and grabs a handful before passing her the bag. He picks it through, tossing the chocolate candy bits one by one into the woods.

"What are you doing? You can't throw the candies into the woods," Catherine says, scrambling around on the ground picking them up and putting them in her jacket pocket.

"What are you doing?" Blake laughs and watches her crawl around the side of the trail retrieving bits of chocolate.

Catherine laughs, realizing how crazy she must look.

"The chocolate bits ruin the mix."

Catherine nods knowingly, "I heard that from someone before."

"I think the squirrels like chocolate," Blake teases.

"I have heard that too, but the squirrels still can't eat the chocolate," Catherine teases back.

Catherine closes up the trail mix and gives it back to Blake as they reach the parking lot.

"I'm over this way," Catherine says, motioning to her car.

"I'm down this way," Blake responds, tilting his head in the other direction.

"Thanks for the company."

"It was a pleasure."

Scratching the dogs and giving them kisses on their head she says, "bye Mason and Annie."

As Catherine packs her things in her car, she looks down the parking lot in Blake's direction and giving him a small wave.

However, when she puts her key in the ignition she realizes her car won't start. Frantically, she checks that the car is in park and tries it again, but still nothing. She pulls out her cell phone to call the auto club but doesn't have any signal. She opens the car door and climbs out and tries different spots to get signal on her phone.

Blake is still there, watching. "Is everything okay? Are you having car trouble?"

"My car won't start. I just had it in the shop. I don't understand why it isn't working," she says, holding her phone up in the air. She avoids eye contact out of embarrassment for her vulnerable position and paces around the lot looking for cell phone signal.

"Toss me your keys and I will take a look."

"Okay," she says, uncomfortably, "but once I get a signal I can just call the auto club and they'll take a look at it."

Blake climbs in the car and tries to start the engine, but it doesn't crank. He pops the hood to look around and says, "I'm already here, why wait on the auto club when it is no trouble for me to give you a jumpstart."

"The mechanic said it was in perfect shape. How could this happen?"

"You probably just left a light on. It happens to everyone now and again."

"I had it tuned up and the oil changed and everything."

"Don't worry about it," Blake says, putting his hand on her shoulder. "I have jumper cables back at home. Come on, we'll get you all fixed up."

Blake opens the passenger door for Catherine and loads the dogs in the bed. As Blake drives down the lane to exit the park, he slows down as they cross over the one lane bridge that crosses over the river. In the center of the bridge he pauses and Catherine sees him looking, just as she always does, back toward the rock outcropping where they had just been sitting.

"Pretty view, isn't it?" Blake asks.

She can sense it is more of a rhetorical question, but the scene melts her stress away. It is hard to feel stressed when taking in the beauty and grandeur of nature. That's what she loves about Falls Park.

"This is my favorite view," Blake says.

She smiles as she is thinking the same thing at that moment.

Blake chuckles, turns up the radio and starts singing along to the familiar tune. As the song changes, he sings along to this one, too. It seems he knows all the country classics.

"I feel lucky…"

"Do you really believe that nonsense?"

"The song? Yeah, I believe it. It's just good for the soul."

"Okay!" She says, laughing it off.

There's something so refreshing and almost magnetic about his outlook. At home there was so much pressure. Everything seemed so stressful and urgent, but here things seem easy.

"Like the song says, I have friends that love me and a

pretty good life. I have a few dollars, my trusty truck, and I'm alive another day. You see, life can be easy or it can be hard, you choose!"

"You make it sound so simple."

"From where I'm sittin' it looks like you have it pretty good."

"Perhaps you don't have a good view from your seat."

"Or maybe you don't see what is right in front of you."

"This is it," Blake announces as they pull into his driveway.

He has a long driveway with a cozy log cabin situated at the end. The back of the property is lined with a thick grove of pine trees. As they get closer, she can see that the cabin is modest in size, and she can't help but notice the attention to detail. The covered porch has a swing and a neatly stacked wood pile. There is a fire pit off to one side and a stamped concrete walkway from the driveway to the front door. He parks in front of what appears to be an oversized garage that is matched perfectly to the style of the cabin.

"I think the cables are in my workshop," he says and hops out of the truck.

Mason and Annie jump out of the truck and chase each other through the yard.

"It is beautiful and peaceful back here with all the trees."

"I have always thought so. Come on, let's go find you those jumper cables."

He opens the huge barn style doors to the garage, revealing his neat and tidy workshop. Catherine was expecting a dirty storage area full of half-finished projects and materials haphazardly strewn about. Instead she finds a perfectly arranged workshop. "Do you always keep everything so organized?"

"I try to! I have the cables in the back. Let me grab them."

She lets her hand glide across his clean workbench admiring how the tools are carefully hung above on a peg board, and everything is in its place, the floors swept so clean you could eat off them.

"I found 'em! We are all set!"

Catherine trips on his stool and tries to grab the workbench to stop her fall and knocks a plastic tray off the edge and covers her head as she hears the sound of pieces hitting the ground.

"Are you ok up there?" Blake asks rushing over to see what happened.

"I'm sorry. You had everything put away so carefully."

"It had to be the 200-piece socket wrench set?"

Blake crouches down to gather the sockets and fit them back into their tray.

"I don't know how I knocked it over. I will fix it."

Blake laughs. "Don't worry about it. I'm just playing. Nothing is broken and it happens all the time."

Catherine looks around again at every tool in its place.

"Really? This happens all the time?"

"No, not really."

Blake takes the sockets from her and dumps them back onto the plastic storage tray and pushes them back on the bench to organize later.

"I just want to grab Annie and Mason some dinner before we get your car fixed up."

"Mason, Annie?" Blake calls as they head into the house.

They step inside and she hears the click clack of their nails as they run across the wood floors and jump up to greet her with puppy hugs. Laughing, she says, "You are too sweet."

Blake puts down their dinner dishes and the dogs quickly forget their love for her.

She finds herself speechless as she takes in the house around her. The log style carries into the house creating the ambience of a warm mountain retreat. The kitchen is small but modern and upgraded with an island and a small table off to one side. The lounge is a large room with a two-story, floor-to-ceiling wood-burning stone fireplace and oversized leather couches that look like the perfect place to curl up for a nap on a cold winter day.

"Your house is so…" but she doesn't finish as she can't think of any word that would describe how warm and welcoming it feels.

"It's home."

Blake grabs a red cooler from the pantry and pulls some cold beers from the fridge, topping them with ice. Then he calls the dogs, and they all head back to the truck.

As they drive back to the park, Catherine finds herself noticing Blake more than she had before. She hadn't missed that he was charming and sexy, but she finds herself intrigued as he seems different than she first thought. She thinks, there is more to him than what she had seen on the surface.

Just then it is like he can sense her looking at him and he asks, "What?"

She blushes a deep red in her cheeks and looks away.

As they enter the park he pulls his truck over next to her car. "Good thing, it isn't summer or there wouldn't be a spot for me to pull near your car."

In the summer the park is crowded with tourists from the city looking for a hike and an afternoon swim. Blake lets the puppies out to run around and hooks up the jumper cables and gets her car going again.

"We should let it run for a few minutes."

She hops up on the tailgate and watches as he tosses the Frisbee with the dogs. She feels so relaxed and finds herself even laughing as she watches them play.

He leaves the dogs and joins her on the tailgate, pulling out 2 beers. He holds one to her.

"I can't, I still have to drive home."

"I think you can have one beer and make it through town and back home in one piece."

Catherine laughs. "Maybe you're right." She accepts and clinks her bottle gently against his, "cheers."

They each take a sip of the beer, watching Mason and Annie grab the Frisbee in a tug of war.

"I may come off like I don't have a care in the world, but my life hasn't been so easy."

Catherine looks down embarrassed.

"Whenever things aren't going my way, I just believe tomorrow is going to be a better day."

"You make it sound so simple."

"Maybe it is."

Catherine nods silently.

"Come on girls. Let's let Catherine get on home!"

He calls the dogs back over to the truck and they hop up into the bed. She pets them and gives them a kiss before they lie down.

"You ok to get home?"

"Yeah, I'll be fine."

"Make sure to turn your headlights off."

"Thanks again for today!" For a moment she doesn't move, she feels hesitant to leave, but isn't sure why.

"Let me help you down," Blake says, holding her hand as she hops off the tailgate.

He watches as she gets into her car, before pulling out of the park.

As she pulls over the one lane bridge she again pauses to take in the last bit of light dancing off the river below, before driving back home.

Chapter 6

The next day, opening the door to the nail salon, the jingle bell wreath announces her arrival. Inside, Catherine admires the twinkle lights and garland decorating the shop. A familiar Christmas carol plays in the background and a tree lights up the front window of the shop.

"Look at you. You are positively radiant," Ginger says, giving Catherine a tight hug, rocking her from side to side.

"Thank you," Catherine says.

She slips off her coat and hangs it on the hook.

"Something is different about you. It's not your hair," Ginger says.

Ginger looks her up and down trying to figure out what has changed.

"What did you do differently?" Ginger asks.

Catherine thinks about her afternoon at Falls Park with Blake, blushes and looks down at her feet.

"I may have met a guy," Catherine admits, smiling from ear to ear. "I don't know though, I mean, I'm not sure. I haven't felt like this in a long time."

"I want to be happy for you, but I can't talk about this now. With my divorce, it's just so hard, you understand how it is," Ginger says.

"I thought you wanted to get divorced. Isn't it a good thing?" Catherine says.

"Maybe, I don't know anymore. How could this be a good thing? Divorce is hard."

Catherine, feeling overwhelmed and trapped by Ginger's chattiness, wonders how she can back out of this girl's day. But at that moment the nail technician grabs her hands and there's no escape.

"I already picked some colors for us. I was thinking rosy pink would be darling on you! And for me this classic red. What do you think?" Ginger asks.

Catherine frowns, thinking to herself, *does this woman ever take a breath?*

"You think the red is too much, don't you?" Ginger says, putting the red polish back.

The nail technician offers them a glass of champagne and adjusts the water temperature in the foot bath.

Ginger turns on the massage chair, slides her feet into the warm water and lets out a sigh.

"I needed this. You cannot imagine what my week was like! I met with my lawyer to draft the divorce papers, and did I tell you about the guy I am seeing?" Ginger says.

Catherine shakes her head no.

"I started seeing this super successful lawyer, Will, a few months back. He is the best in the business and so hand-some. Quite a catch."

"So what's the problem?" Catherine asks.

"He doesn't know I'm still married," Ginger says.

"Why don't you just tell him?" Catherine suggests.

"I'm not sure how he'll take the news. He is the most

eligible bachelor in the state, and I don't want to risk losing him."

Catherine finds herself daydreaming and wishing she was back on the tailgate of Blake's truck laughing and drinking a beer.

"Hello? Catherine, did you even hear a word of what I was saying?" Ginger asks.

"I'm sorry I just missed some of it," Catherine says.

"I mean, do you think it's lying? It's not really lying."

"Well, we all have our secrets."

Suddenly Catherine is nervous about what she wasn't telling Blake. Would he be scared away if he knew about Aleksandra?

Ginger continued on without encouragement. "I'm not sure if I should go through with this. How will I handle everything on my own? I can't have a baby on my own. I don't even know if Will, the lawyer I'm dating, is ready to get married."

Catherine wants to tell Ginger she can do it alone, but she wonders what would have been different, if she had shared the experience of having a child with someone she loved. She understands why Ginger wants to be married again. *Maybe I should have opened up more and let love in.* The whole conversation has Catherine's head spinning.

Back home, she steps inside the mudroom and hears Blake's radio playing music and walks to the doorway where she can see him working in the living room. He has his back to her and is measuring and making marks on a piece of wood. She smiles, liking the feeling of him in her house. She sits down to take her shoes off and notices something missing. Where are Aleksandra's boots? They always sat in this spot next to the door. How many times had Catherine reminded her to put her boots next to the door and reprimanded her saying, "Don't track all that mud from the barn through the house!"

She opens the coat closet and they aren't there. She shuts the closet door and gets down on her hands and knees frantically searching in the dark beneath the bench. She is crouched down with her cheek on the cold tile reaching back and forth longing to find them. She feels hot tears beginning to sting her eyes. Her breath becomes shallow and she hops up and races down the hall to look in Aleksandra's bedroom.

She throws open the door and finds all the lights on. The furniture has been removed from the room and the carpet is pulled back. There is a tray of fresh paint and a brush wrapped in cellophane in the corner. She is feeling lightheaded. She throws open the closet and sees all of her things missing, and in her hurry to leave the bedroom she walks into Blake.

"Whoa, where are you headed in such a rush?" he asks.

"What are you doing to her room?" She asks, motioning to the work in Aleksandra's bedroom.

Blake stares at her, confused.

One tear escapes and starts to slowly run down her cheek. "I can't find her boots," she says.

"Her boots?" he questions.

"Yes, where are her riding boots?"

He stares at her blankly.

"They weren't in the mudroom, and they aren't in her room. Where are they?" she asks.

"I didn't see any boots." Blake says.

"They're gone," she gasped.

"What did I do wrong? I wanted to surprise you. I

thought you would be happy, I never expected it would upset you," Blake explains.

"Just think, where did you move them to?" she asks.

"I don't know, but I am sure we can find them."

"I want to be alone right now. Please."

She steps back into Aleksandra's room and gently shuts the door behind her. She turns in a circle, taking in all of her now naked room. She closes her eyes and can see where it once had horse pictures and ribbons tacked to the walls. On the far wall was her vanity, usually a mess with makeup strewn all over.

She sits down in the room and remembers the last weekend she slept here. They had played with the horses until after dark and left in a rush to get home and get ready for the week. As they raced out of the house that weekend, she never expected that Aleksandra's things would sit here, never to be touched by her again.

She stands up taking one last look around the room. She had thought she was ready for the renovations, but maybe she isn't for the changes. It doesn't feel like her anymore. It just feels empty. She opens the door and sees Blake quietly waiting in the hallway, holding the boots. He holds them out to her and she leans into his arms letting the tears flow. Blake hugs her closely, comforting her and wiping her tears with the sleeve of his shirt.

She looks up at Blake, wishing she had the words to explain how she wasn't ready to change their home like she thought, but maybe he knows.

Catherine puts on her jacket and boots and wanders down the path to the barn to check on Tinka and Breezy. For years, they had trailered the horses with them on every visit to the lake. Aleksandra had lessons at home, but wanted to ride when away at the lake, too.

After last year, having the horses at home was too

painful for her. Nelly had made arrangements with their friends at Fox Run Stables. They sent one of their stable hands and trailered them up to the lake house. Once there, he now manages all of their day to day needs, from feeding and farriers, to vet visits.

"Hey Sam. How are my girls?" Catherine asks.

"I was just going to put them out to play while I clean their stalls!" Sam answers.

"Can I help you?" Catherine asks.

She finds a lead rope and attaches it to Tinka's halter and leads her out to the paddock while Sam follows behind with Breezy. Rubbing Tinka's neck, she gives her a kiss on the forehead as she takes off the lead rope and closes the gate behind them.

She grabs a flake of hay and puts it in the hay rack on the side of the stall, checks the water bucket and sees that it is full of clean water. Then she brushes Tinka down before putting on the saddle pad and saddle. Once she finishes, she sees an apple on the way out and takes it back to Tinka as a treat. She turns to pick up the saddle and sees Blake walking down the path through the yard.

"You ride?" Catherine asks, seeing him approach.

"A little."

"I was just getting ready to take her for a ride."

"Can I join you?"

"Aren't you supposed to be working?" she teases.

"I don't think the boss will mind a short break," he jokes.

They get the other horse, Breezy, tacked up and Catherine leads the way to a trail across the street. They head into a wooded area and ride in silence through a forest of old maple and oak trees. They ride in silence as they follow a path across a stream, until they come to a field that looks like an old orchard.

"I have never been back here," Blake says.

"It is one of my favorite spots."

Catherine climbs down from her horse and tethers the horses to a low hanging branch of an apple tree.

"I remember one summer day, a few years back, when my daughter Aleksandra and I took a ride back here. We saw some bears eating apples that had fallen from these trees and Tinka got spooked and threw Aleksandra off. I was panicked and raced over to where she was lying in the grass and found her laughing. She wasn't hurt or even scared."

"She sounds brave."

"She was, and she loved horses. Every morning she would wake up and race down to the barn to say good morning. She would wrap her arms around Tinka, resting her cheek on her neck and whisper quietly to her while petting the front of her nose and showering her with kisses. I am not sure what they talked about but it seemed to soothe her."

"When did she fall in love with horses?" Blake asked.

"She was probably six or seven when I signed up for some lessons. She was riding Tinka, and the barn owner told me she was for sale, so I bought her. I was worried about how much work it would be to care for a horse, but Aleksandra took such good care of her. She would gently lift her leg to clean her hooves and carefully loosen and comb all the dirt out of her fur and then brush and braid her mane and tail. I think she would have moved her bed into the barn if I let her."

Blake takes Catherine by the hand and walks with her to an open part of the field and finds a sun spot for them to sit in the grass.

"I thought you were a city girl in love with all that hustle and bustle?"

"That's just work!" She lays back in the grass with her hands behind her head looking up at the sky.

Blake joins her lying down on his back next to her.

"I love it out here with the blue skies, puffy white clouds, and the smell of the fresh air!" Catherine says.

"I agree, it is pretty out here," Blake says.

"What do you think that one looks like?" Catherine says, pointing up at a cloud.

"Maybe a rabbit? What do you see?"

Catherine twists her head trying to see the cloud from his perspective.

"I can't tell," Catherine says.

"See this part over here? I think those are its ears and that part over there is its tail," Blake says.

"I see it now."

They sit in silence, enjoying the sun on their faces and searching for cloud animals.

"My daughter, Aleksandra, died a little over a year ago."

He reaches over for her hand and weaves his fingers through hers.

"I kind of suspected. It is a small town and people talk."

"I am worried that I am forgetting her. I want to remember everything I can about her."

"It's ok, I'm here."

"I miss her and I guess I came back here hoping to find her."

"Did you? Find her, I mean," Blake asks.

"I think I am starting to," Catherine says.

She looks up at the clouds and closes her eyes. Relaxed and breathing in the fresh air, this moment reminds her of how she used to feel when she was with Aleksandra. She feels almost like herself, even if it is just for a minute.

Blake stands up and then offers Catherine his hands and pulls her up. She brushes the dirt off her jeans and mounts Tinka, and Blake hops on Breezy and they walk, each lost in their own thoughts as they head back through the woods and across the stream, back to the barn.

Chapter 7

It is a sunny but cold morning outside. Catherine slips into her wool Fair Isle sweater, and pulls on her mud boots before heading down the path to the barn. The wind still bites Catherine's face, and even as she shelters herself in behind the immense stable door, she can still see her breath.

She grabs the tack box and grooming bin and slides open the stall door and greets Tinka by rubbing her back as she walks up to her head, getting ready to groom her. Catherine feels calm just being in the presence of Tinka, but she also feels the loss of Aleksandra so deeply when with her. *How can I be with you and not Aleksandra?* She thinks to herself.

She tacks Tinka and attaches a lead rope to her halter, leading her into the ring. Then she sees them approaching. The rising sun hasn't warmed her up yet, and a chill slips down her spine. Tinka swishes her tail back and forth in excitement as the little girl of 6 or 7 years skips over towards her.

"This is Tinka. What is your name?" Catherine asks.

"I'm Bella," the little girl says.

"It's so nice to meet you, Bella. Do you want to pet Tinka?" Catherine asks.

Catherine pulls the mounting block next to Tinka and holds Bella's hand as she climbs up the steps.

"She loves when you scratch right here on her neck," Catherine says.

Tinka snorts and Bella pulls her hand back.

"That sound means she's happy," Catherine says.

Catherine picks up Bella's hand and shows her again how to stroke Tinka's neck.

"She's so furry."

"Yes, she gets furrier in the winter. It keeps her warm!"

Catherine looks at Bella, remembering when Aleksandra first met Tinka. She had been a little older, but she had that same look in her eyes.

"Would you like to ride her around the ring?"

Catherine tightens up the stirrups and helps Bella up and then guides her around the ring, nice and slow.

"Again, Again! Let's do it again!"

Catherine helps Bella hop down and takes off Tinka's lead rope.

"I think Tinka loves this attention. It has been a while since she had a little girl love her like this."

"Shall we go talk to your Mommy and Daddy?"

"Mommy, Daddy, I love her. Can I take her home? Pleeeeaaaaassssseeee!"

"She's beautiful, isn't she, Bella?" Her mother says.

"Mommy, she is so soft. Did you pet her?"

"No, I didn't pet her."

"C'mon you have to come pet her!" Bella drags her Mommy back over to where Tinka is standing.

Catherine watches Bella giggling excitedly and hugging Tinka.

Aleksandra had been seven years old when she brought Tinka home. She took care of Tinka like she was her baby. Grooming her and feeding her and mucking her stall and riding her nearly every day. She never tired of it. Sometimes Catherine would find Aleksandra in the barn sitting in Tinka's stall, studying. Aleksandra talked about how she was going to pick her college based on where she could board Tinka. She didn't ever want to part from her. Catherine dreaded the day she would have to comfort Aleksandra as she said goodbye to her first love. She never imagined that she would be comforting Tinka in her loneliness from losing Aleksandra. She knows it is best if Tinka had a new little girl to love.

Catherine turns around to see Blake walking down, and she feels her heart skip a beat. "Smells like winter is on its way," Blake says.

Catherine looks at him quizzically.

"The air. Can't you just smell the snow coming?" Blake says.

Catherine takes a deep breath. "I just smell horses," she says.

"It is easy to miss, but the first snow is one of my favorite days of the year."

"Do you need me for anything?"

"No, I just saw you down here and thought I would stop down to say good morning. I'm sorry, I didn't mean to interrupt your riding lesson."

"No, I am not teaching a lesson. Actually, they are here to buy Tinka."

"You're selling your horse?"

"That's the plan."

"That's crazy. You can't sell your horse."

"I can't? I don't remember asking for your permission."

"Of course you don't need permission. What I meant was that you love your horses."

Catherine scowls and walks over to the mom and dad and Bella.

"Isn't she sweet?"

"She seems sweet but I think she might be too much horse for Bella," her father muttered.

"Sure, I understand. At 16 hands, Tinka can seem like a giant compared to a little girl," Catherine responds. "But she is gentle and perfect for an amateur like your daughter. Not to mention, she has been through years of training and is very experienced. She loves lessons as much as she loves trail rides. In the summer her favorite thing to do is go for a swim in the lake!"

"She swims?" Bella squeals.

"Uh-huh, she loves to go for a walk down our beach over there and then swim in the lake when she's hot!"

Catherine recalls how much Aleksandra would take Tinka on long walks and swims at the ocean. She did English lessons and dressage for a bit as well. She did jumping and Tinka was steady and athletic. She realizes they are asking her a question, but she wasn't really listening.

"Oh, yes, she really is a great fit for your young daughter to love. If you would like we can put her on Tinka and lead her around the ring a few times."

Blake notices Catherine seems distracted and distant. "Let

me help you put her up in the saddle," he says and follows Catherine over to Tinka.

He leans close to Catherine so the family wouldn't hear. "Don't do this! You don't know what you're doing."

"Just stay out of it."

Catherine takes Bella by the hand to lead her over to the mounting block to help her get up on Tinka. Her plastered smile at the family makes Blake laugh.

She hoists Bella in her arms, when Blake walks up behind Tinka, quietly, where she can't see or hear him, and then he smacks Tinka's hind quarters.

Everyone is stunned as Tinka rears up to twice the height of the adults, before running off in the opposite direction. The father steals his daughter from Catherine's arms, and Catherine stares, fuming at Blake.

"You ok?" Blake asks, attempting to calm her.

She spins on her heal attending to the family. "Is Bella okay? Tinka doesn't usually startle easily! Blake walked up behind her, and she didn't know he was there and got spooked."

"I'm ok. Is Tinka ok?" Bella asks.

"Yes, she just got scared," Catherine explains.

"She really is beautiful, but just not the right horse for Bella. We just can't risk Bella getting trampled or thrown off. It wouldn't be safe. I'm sure you understand. Come on honey, we need to go," Bella's mom says.

"Nooo, I don't want to go! I want to take Tinka home!" Bella cries.

Catherine watches the family go before turning around to Blake.

"How could you? What were you thinking? That little girl could have gotten hurt."

"She was never in harm's way, and I was just trying to help you."

"What makes you think you have the right to make decisions in my life?"

Catherine rips off her gloves, throwing them down as she walks towards the house.

Blake calls after her, "you are making a big mistake. The other day you were distraught over a pair of riding boots. How do you think you are going to feel when her horse is gone?"

Catherine turns and takes a step back towards Blake, "I can't live like this any longer. It is time for me to clean up this mess and put all this behind me."

"You know, you can't just throw the baby out with the bath water."

Catherine snorts in disgust, "that doesn't even deserve a response."

Blake touches her arm. "You can't just run away from this."

"There is nothing here." Catherine grabs her gloves from Blake's hands. "I am paying you to fix my house, not run my life, and now I don't even want you doing that. I want you to get your tools and get out of here! You're fired."

Chapter 8

Catherine wakes up to the sound of Tinka playing outside. She gets up from bed, throws on her robe, pulls back the curtain from the window, and watches Tinka play. She sees Tinka rolling on her back in the dirt of the riding ring and then she stands up and trots around shaking her head and neighing. She feels lighter and is grateful that she didn't sell her. Then the phone rings, Nelly is calling to check on her.

Nelly is obnoxiously upbeat and asks how she is.

"How am I? My house is a mess and I feel like this renovation will never be finished, much less on schedule. I only have a few more weeks to get things done," Catherine says.

"Blake seems to have things under control, and I am sure he will get it done on time," Nelly says.

She pulls back the tarp blocking the dust from traveling upstairs and steps into the living room. She sees two ladders set up, one on each side of the room and a table saw in the center of her living room. Paint trays, buckets, and tools are scattered around the room. *What a mess*, Catherine thinks to herself.

"I kind of fired him yesterday," she admits.

"Why would you do that?" Nelly asks.

"He caused a huge scene and it messed up the sale of Tinka," Catherine says.

"Is it possible, he was trying to help you?" Nelly asks.

"I really don't want to talk about it," Catherine says with a sigh.

"I think, it is time to talk about this. It is time you let people help you and stop trying to do everything on your own," Nelly says.

"It was none of his business," Catherine says.

"That's my point. It isn't his business, but he still cared enough about you to try and save you from making a decision you would regret for a long time. How can you not see this?" Nelly says.

Catherine sighs, not feeling ready to trust him or let him into her life.

"You need to fix this. Go talk to him and get him back," Nelly says.

Catherine hangs up the phone and sinks down to the floor taking in the mess around her. *What would I even say to Blake after my outburst yesterday?* She thinks to herself.

A few hours later, she pulls up to Blake's cabin and finds herself ringing his doorbell.

"What are you doing here?" Blake asks.

"Peace offering?" Catherine says, holding up the beers she picked up at the corner market on the way to his house.

"Want to come in?" Blake offers.

"Look, I realize I may have overreacted a bit the other day, and I'm sorry."

"It's fine, don't worry about it," Blake says.

"No, it's not fine. I know you are doing great work on my house and I want to thank you," Catherine says. Blake steps aside, as she brushes past him, awkwardly entering his cabin.

"That's it? You drove over here to thank me for my work?"

"Of course!"

Blake shakes his head in disbelief. "How am I not surprised?" he says.

"I'm trying to apologize and you are just blowing me off," Catherine says.

"Actually, I'm really busy right now. I have to get this float finished and I don't have time for this today."

"Float?"

"For the Holly Berry Festival. Every year I make the sleigh for Santa and Mrs. Clause to ride in on."

"Oh well, I'm sorry to bother you."

"Do you want to see it?"

Catherine nods and Blake takes her into his workshop. The base of the float is covered in white sheeting to look like snow, with a giant sleigh on top. The body of the sleigh is painted red with gold runners. Surrounding the sleigh are miniature evergreen trees in burlap sacks with white twinkle lights.

"I'm going to add some snowflake details on the sides of the sleigh and put twinkle lights on the runners," Blake says, tracing the edge of his carpentry with a finger.

"Wow, it's so beautiful," Catherine says.

"You seem surprised," Blake says.

"I'm not surprised, it's just really beautiful. When did you have any time to work on this?" Catherine asks, admiring his work.

"How are you with a paintbrush? I could use some help painting," Blake says.

Catherine puts on an apron, grabs a paintbrush, and starts adding a second coat of gold to the sleigh runners, while Blake stencils the snowflake details on the sides.

"I meant, what I said before. I am really happy with your work. I want you to come back and finish."

"I'll have to think about it," Blake teases.

"I understand if you don't want to come back," Catherine says disappointedly, "but I hope you can at least forgive me for how I blew up at you."

Blake flicks his paint brush splattering her hair with paint.

"What are you doing?" Catherine asks.

"You need to lighten up and have some fun," Blake says and flicks the paint brush at her again.

"I will show you how to have fun. Remember you asked for it, Mister!"

Catherine ducks down behind her side of the sleigh and dips her brush into the gold paint and quietly walks towards the back of the sleigh, peaking around the edge. She watches, waiting for him to turn around, and when he does she splatters him with the gold paint.

"Now, look at what you did!" Blake says, pointing out the gold paint that landed on the finished sleigh.

"Oh no, I am so sorry!" Catherine says, looking around for some paper towels. She tries to wipe the paint off, smearing the gold paint, making it more noticeable.

Blake laughs, watching her make a bigger mess out of the paint.

He puts his arm around her shoulder, "It is no big deal. It's ok, we were just having fun. You worry too much!"

Catherine realizes he had only been pretending to be upset about the paint splatter, flicks him again with her paintbrush, splattering paint to his face, before running to hide behind the sleigh.

"Truce. I call a truce," Blake says from his hiding spot on the other side of the sleigh.

They're laughing again by the time they clean up the paint cans and wash out the brushes.

"I was going to make some stew for dinner. Would you want to stay and maybe join me?" Blake asks.

Catherine thinks about the fun she had with Blake working on the float and feels intrigued to know more about him.

"I'd love to!"

"The renovations to your place are coming along nicely. And on schedule, I might add," Blake says.

"Hopefully someone will be able to ring in the New Year in their newly renovated home," Catherine says.

"You aren't going to stay through the holidays?" Blake asks.

"No, I need to get back home and get back to work and real life."

"You know real life happens here, too."

Blake rummages through the refrigerator, piling his arms with the carrots, celery, potatoes, onions, and beef and piles them on the island. He grabs knives and cutting boards, before going to the pantry for the flour and spices and a pot.

Catherine separates the ingredients and starts chopping the onions.

"Can I offer you a beer?" he suggests, opening her peace offering and handing her one.

"So, you never wanted to move away from here?" Catherine asks.

Blake picks up a potato and starts to peel and cut it. "Actually, when I was younger, I had planned to go away for college. I was accepted at University of North Carolina and my girlfriend Jennifer was, too. We had this dream to go away and study. Then, in the spring of our senior year of high school, we found out she was pregnant. On top of that, her dad accepted a job as a plant manager in Minnesota and they were relocating right after graduation. A lot of people thought I should do right by her and propose, but it didn't feel right. If she moved with her parents, they could help her during her pregnancy and when the baby arrived."

He looks down at the counter as he gets to this part of his story, and Catherine thinks it is touching how he almost blushes.

"There was never any question for her about her plans to raise the baby," he continued. "And I knew we couldn't do that on our own at 19. I would have to work all the time and she would be home alone with the baby all the time. It felt like way too much on us at such a young age, and her parents were so supportive, it made sense to let her go."

"It sounds like you really loved her. It must have been hard."

Blake puts the peeler down, thinking back on that time.

"After graduation I said good bye and I got to work straight away. I didn't want to be one of those dads. I sent everything I earned to them, and whenever I had a break in jobs, I would drive out there to see her and Zach. Her parents always welcomed me to stay with them. After a while, I thought about moving there, but when Zach was a few years old, Jennifer got married."

"I don't think a lot of guys would be so welcoming towards a guy marrying the woman they love," Catherine says.

"He really loved her and Zach. I know she did all the work in raising him, but I tried to be there as much as I could."

"Wow, what's he doing now?"

"Zach's 37 and lives right down the road from his mama, but we still talk and see each other as often as we can. He's a real smart kid and he is doing really well for himself. He's running a hugely successful business and traveling the world. She did a good job raising him!"

Catherine notices the collage of pictures on the refrigerator and asks, "is that him? He is almost as handsome as his dad! Did you ever regret not marrying her?"

"When she first got married I did, but we were so young. She had her hands full and I was working nonstop to support her. There wasn't time for love or romance in those years. We're good friends. I see her when I go visit Zach, and it's good this way," Blake says.

"Well, I told you all about me. What about you? What happened between you and Aleksandra's dad?"

"Um. Same. I was young and working nonstop. What did you say before? There was no time for romance or love!"

"That's not fair. I told you about me. There must have been someone?"

"Just my firm," Catherine says. "Actually, I was engaged once, but it didn't work out. After that I decided to have a baby on my own and focus on her and my work."

"Work is good, but we all need something more, you know, something that really keeps your soul alive and makes your heart happy."

"Do you have that?"

"Still looking," Blake says with a wink.

"You know you weren't entirely wrong the other day. I realize I can't do this all on my own."

"Was that a real apology I just heard?" Blake winks at her.

Catherine watches as Blake picks up the dishes.

"How is it that some girl hasn't already scooped you up?" Catherine asks.

"It's been complicated," Blake says.

"Now look, who's not sharing."

He gives her a mischievous smile. "It's not every day you meet someone special that could change the direction of your life."

Catherine blushes. "It's getting late, I should get going."

"Did I scare you away?"

Catherine laughs, getting up from her chair. "I just really should be going."

Moments later in her car, Catherine feels a smile spread across her face and she tries to remember the last time being with a man left her feeling giddy.

Chapter 9

Back at home, Catherine listens to the sound of the fire crackling and looks out the living room picture window onto the fresh blanket of snow. She wonders if there is anything more peaceful than staring off into an abyss of fluffy white flakes... It is the perfect afternoon for fuzzy socks and her favorite sweater, and to curl up with a warm blanket for a lazy afternoon with a hot cup of tea and a good book.

She looks over at the bookshelf in the corner and sees an old photo album. There are pictures of Aleksandra as a baby and as a toddler. There is one of her first time on skates! She is bundled up in her snow pants and jacket and big fluffy hat with a pom-pom on top. She is standing on the ice wearing her skates and a big smile. In the photo you can see the snowflakes falling. The only way to cajole Aleksandra off her skates was with a promise of a cookie and a hot chocolate inside. Even on a cold winter day her daughter was always playful and laughing, not complaining. She continues to flip through the album and pulls out a photo of them together from her last birthday with Aleksandra. She traces the image of them dressed up and laughing at a restaurant. She closes her eyes remembering that birthday, when she hears the laughter outside and looks out the window to see kids heading down to the frozen lake for ice skating.

She can hear the chatter of their parents watching nearby. If Aleksandra was here, they would be down on the ice with the neighbors. Aleksandra would skate, and she would talk to the parents and share her homemade cocoa and fresh baked cookies.

She isn't just sad to be missing this moment with Aleksandra, she's angry all over again that she was taken too soon. It isn't fair that she was taken from her life and she is left alone to watch life pass by from the sidelines. She hears the doorbell ring and pushes the photo album under the blanket, and goes answer it. She opens the door to Blake on her front step with some ice skates.

"Join me out on the ice?" Blake asks.

"I don't know, it's been a long time," Catherine says.

"Go get bundled up and meet me down on the ice. I'm not taking no for an answer," Blake says.

Catherine puts some hot cocoa in a thermos and packs up a basket of the fresh baked cookies and layers up in her scarf and coat and hat, before heading down to the lake. Blake is out on the ice, skating like an expert and playing with the kids. She shuffles out onto the ice, tilts her head back, and breathes in the fresh winter air.

She skates around slowly and is surprised when Blake grabs a free hockey stick and joins the kids' game. He spots the boy with the puck, distracts him in a playful body check, and steals it. He quickly skates away to the other goal and scores. Blake childishly pumps his arms in the air in celebration, then skates over to Catherine.

"Blake's got a girlfriend," the little boy teases.

"Awwwww," the other little kids sing in chorus while making kissy noises.

"Did you see my goal?" he asks Catherine proudly.

"I saw you steal a puck from a twelve-year-old kid," Catherine teases.

Blake grabs her hands. "Come on, let's skate out to the middle. It's the best view of the mountains."

As they skate towards the middle her legs warm up and soon she glides along the ice smoothly. Away from the noise of the kids and families playing at the edge of the lake, the center is peaceful and quiet. All she can hear is the "swoosh" of her skates gripping the ice. Blake takes her hands and shows her how to skate backwards and do a spin, like they are on a dance floor, not the frozen lake.

"It looks the sun is starting to go down. How about we go back for some of that cocoa you made?" Blake suggests.

They find a quiet spot with a log to sit on and enjoy their hot cocoa and watch the parents collecting their kids to go home.

"These kids out here playing hockey remind me of my winters here as a kid. My brothers and I would race out to the lake first thing in the morning and skate until dark fell."

"Are you still close with your brothers?"

"We're really close. I get to play cool Uncle Blake with my brother's kids. That was my nephew I stole the puck from."

"I think my family was a little more uptight than yours."

"You don't say? I never would have guessed," Blake laughs.

Catherine gives him a playful shove. "When we went out, my mom would instruct me, Catherine, no standing on your head! Catherine, a lady always crosses her ankles, not her knees! Catherine, a young woman rests her hands gently in her lap!"

"Everything is making sense now," Blake says, still laughing.

"Hearing myself say that out loud, I realize it does sound a bit silly. Maybe life doesn't need to be so controlled and perfect," Catherine says.

"You are fun like this," Blake says.

"Look, it is starting to snow again!" Catherine says excitedly.

She stands up and skates out from the shelter of the tree to feel the snow. She laughs, enjoying the snow falling on her lashes, wet and cold. Catherine goes to skate further onto the lake and hits a bump in the ice and falls. Blake scoops her up into his arms and holds her close. Shivering, she tucks her head down into his shoulder, and she can feel his breath on her neck. She looks up at Blake, and he takes his scarf off and wraps it around her neck.

"You're freezing," Blake says. "Let's get you warmed up."

With his arm around her he leads her off the ice and back up to the house.

"I know you don't eat much," Blake teases, "but I stopped by the market on the way here and got some steaks for dinner. Go get warmed up and I will cook these for us."

Surprised, Catherine enjoys the feeling of someone taking care of her. She takes her time getting changed and finding something cozy to bundle up in. From the foot of the stairs she watches him for a moment outside on the deck, grilling as the snow is gently falling. She grabs a bottle of wine, some glasses, and her blanket, before going out on the deck to join him. The porch swing is near the patio heater, but still as she unfurls the blanket to wrap herself up, a picture from the album falls to the ground. Blake picks it up and brushes off the snow.

"She's pretty," Blake says, handing the picture back to her.

Catherine looks at the picture and closes her eyes momentarily. "This picture was taken on my last birthday with her. I don't remember the last time I laughed like that!" Catherine says.

"I remember, that night she was telling me about a boy in her civics class who was always hungry. He brought a hot dog for lunch and had it in the pocket of his hoodie. During class he would wait until the teacher wasn't looking and he would duck down and stuff a huge piece of the hot dog into his mouth and chew it with his mouth open, smacking and dropping hot dog crumbs all over his desk. You had to be there when she was telling the story. It was much funnier when she acted it out than when I tell the story."

The tears slowly and softly run down her cheeks as she remembers their time together. Blake joins her on the porch swing and holds her hand and gently rocks the swing.

"I miss her every day. I don't know how to laugh like that without her. I don't know how to be without her. Most nights, I want to forget her because it hurts so much, but most days, I worry that I might forget her and try to remember everything I can about her. I came here hoping to find her."

He moves closer and puts his arm around her and holds her.

"Shhh, it's ok. It's all going to be ok. I'm here with you now," Blake says.

Her crying slows down and she rests her head on his shoulder, relaxing into the comfort of his presence. They sit in silence for a long time until Blake says, thoughtfully, "I know you miss her every day and I can never know what that feels like for you, but I believe she chose you as her mom for a reason."

He gently glides the swing again before going on.

"If you go through every day feeling the emptiness and tragedy of losing her, then you will stay trapped in your pain. If you can celebrate her and share the gifts she brought you, then you will release yourself from this pain."

They sit together outside in quiet, watching the full moon reflecting off the ice on the frozen lake. Somehow she's ready to breathe again, and to listen, because she finally feels heard.

He gives her a gentle hug and kisses the top of her head.

She turns and looks up at him taking in his kind and gentle green eyes. His lips softly brush against her cheek and she turns towards him, welcoming him as his lips gently press against her lips. She wonders if he can hear how loudly her heart is beating against his as she relaxes into his arms. She turns towards him, drawing him closer to her, wanting more of him. She breathes in his sweet smell and enjoys the feeling of his beard brushing along her face, reminding her that she is alive. His lips feel so warm against hers, and she doesn't want to open her eyes for fear this moment will end.

She hears him whisper, "you're shivering, let's get you inside." He scoops her up in his arms and carries her inside to the couch. She sinks into the oversized sofa, as Blake covers her with a blanket.

"Let me go pour us some wine."

Catherine wakes on the couch, alone, to the sun streaming

in the windows. She checks her watch, 9 AM. For the first time since losing Aleksandra she has slept all night. She feels rested and somehow lighter. She goes into the kitchen and sees a note on the counter. Blake scrawled "Sweet dreams, Catherine. XO."

Chapter 10

Catherine walks to the Lakeside Boutique Boutique with the giddiness of a young girl, eager to find the perfect outfit for the Holly Berry Festival. The silence of the morning is both beautiful and peaceful. Perfect for a winter walk.

As she walks the wind blows gently and snow falls softly from the tree branches. In the fields along the road she can see the hoof prints from where deer had been dancing last night.

She skips into the Lakeside Boutique and smiles warmly at the saleswoman in the store. As soon as she starts sifting through the racks, the door opens behind her bringing in a cold gust of air. The saleswoman brushes past Catherine, rushing to excitedly greet the woman. "Ginger! I can't believe you are finally here! Get over here and give me a hug."

Ginger! Catherine thinks to herself and ducks behind the nearest clothing rack, hoping she doesn't see her.

Ginger greets the saleswoman with her usual enthusiasm, "I was running late, but here now!" She tells the saleswoman about her harrowing drive through the mountains in the snow and ice, until her friend cuts her off, "have you seen him yet?"

"Not yet!"

"The parade is tonight!"

"I know! The Christmas spirit and some hot cocoa will be the perfect atmosphere."

The women walk around the rack and see Catherine crouched down. Catherine, not knowing what to do, digs through the rack with knees bent and announces, "Found it!"

The saleswoman seems convinced. "I'm so sorry! I didn't even introduce myself. I haven't seen my girlfriend in so long. I'm sure you understand how that is. Anyway, I'm Aubrey, and welcome to the Lakeside Boutique!" Catherine smiles and waves at Ginger.

Ginger scoops Catherine in a hug, rocking her back and forth.

"I am so happy to see you! I've been trying to call you for days! I thought maybe you were mad at me," Ginger exclaims.

"Oh, of course not. I've just been real busy," Catherine says.

"What are you looking for today?" Aubrey asks.

"I'm not sure...," as she nervously picks through the racks.

"What's the occasion? A party, or girl's night, or maybe a date?" Aubrey asks.

"I'm not sure. Maybe it's a date?" Catherine says, grabbing a few things from the rack to try on.

"That's the best kind!" Ginger interrupts. "We are going to make sure it's a date and the best night of his life!"

She grabs the clothes Catherine has picked up and vetoes all of them.

"Where are the two of you going on your date?" Aubrey asks, eyeing her from head to toe.

"We are going to the Holly Berry Festival, but I am not sure it's a date," Catherine says.

Ginger holds up a tiny black dress to Catherine and says, "You need something like this to show off those curves."

"I agree that would be flattering, but not sure that dress will do for the festival," Aubrey says. She takes a step back to assess Catherine's figure and think about what would be just right.

Catherine crosses her arms over her chest, feeling exposed with the stares of Aubrey and Ginger.

"Is your new guy coming to the festival?" Catherine asks Ginger.

"I'm keeping my options open," Ginger says.

"I thought he was the one?" Catherine questions.

"Don't you worry about me, honey! I've got all the men beating down my door!" Ginger says.

"Let's get Catherine ready for her date," Aubrey suggests.

"It's obvious you have been out of the dating game a while. Don't worry, you are at the right place, because Aubrey and I are going to fix you up and you are going to knock his socks off!" Ginger says.

Catherine turns around to the nearest rack and finds a pair of Khaki slacks and picks them off the rack and holds them up to herself checking out her reflection in the mirror. Ginger snatches the pants out of Catherine's hands.

"Do you work at Target?" Ginger asks, horrified.

"What are you talking about? These are nice pants," Catherine says.

Ginger puts the pants back randomly on the rack.

Catherine then picks out a long chunky sweater and Ginger slaps her hand.

"That would be a great if you were going to work in the library," Ginger says.

"Ginger, knock it off. I'm the expert. Don't worry dear, I'll handle this," Aubrey says.

Aubrey comes back with a fitted red top and some black leggings and points her towards the dressing room.

"That's just what she needs to show off that ass," Ginger laughs, slapping Catherine's ass, and shuts the dressing room door behind her.

In the privacy of the dressing room, Catherine lets out a sigh. She isn't sure how she feels about Aubrey or Ginger picking her outfit, but they do have a point about the items she was picking out. *Isn't it what's inside that counts?* Catherine thinks, as she struggles to pull on the tight leggings and fitted sweater.

"Get out here and show us how you look!" Ginger says.

Catherine opens the dressing room hesitantly, not realizing how deep the v neck went until she caught her reflection in the mirror.

Ginger lets out a whistle. "Damn! That is much more like it! You look amazing!"

"You do look amazing!" Aubrey agrees.

"We've gotta boost those babies up," says Ginger, reaching over to push Catherine's chest up, exposing more of her cleavage in the V neck. Catherine smacks her away.

"He's seen how I look and I think he likes me. Do I really need all of this?" she asks, pointing at the sexy outfit.

"We don't have much time, so we can't explain about girls and boys grown up feelings right now. What are you going to do with your hair?" Aubrey asks.

"Oh no, you were going to leave it in the ponytail, weren't you?" Ginger says.

"What's wrong with my hair?"

"Ponytails are for the gym, not dates!" Ginger replies.

"I'm calling my sister, Lizzie! She will do your hair and makeup and have you all ready for your date in no time," Aubrey says, already dialing the phone and making arrangements.

Catherine looks at her reflection in the three way mirror and turns to see all angles, feeling ridiculous in this outfit, but these women seemed like the type that know all about men. She hadn't been lucky in this department, so maybe they're right.

Chapter 11

The Holly Berry Festival is the biggest event of the season. Everyone in town gathers to watch the parade and enjoy the start of the holiday season. Lights are strung from the lamp posts and carolers sing outside the shops. Shopkeepers keep their stores open late and everyone enjoys the festive feeling and opportunity to get a jump start on their holiday shopping.

Catherine is excited to see Blake's float before the parade starts. Once the festivities began he would be in the middle of the action, bringing Santa, Mrs. Holly Berry and all the snow princesses to the center of town to light the Christmas tree.

She spots Blake and he waves her over, at which point she almost trips over the high heels of her new boots. "What are you wearing? What's with the stretch pants?" he laughs offering her his coat.

Catherine blushes. "The ladies at the shop today said they made me look hot," she replies, laughing nervously.

"You look hot because you are hot," he says as he pulls her in close, leaning in to kiss her.

"Blake, we need to hook the float up and be ready to roll in 5 minutes," some guy calls out.

"Hold that thought until after the parade?" Blake asks.

"It looks great," Catherine says, tracing her fingers along the snowflake detailing he painted on the side and sees the gold splotch from their paint fight and smiles. "You left it?" she asks.

"I thought it added something special to the design. I think it might be the best float I have made yet," Blake says.

"Meet me by the tree after the parade?" Blake says with a wink.

Catherine smiles and flushes with excitement, "I would love that. Good luck," and she gives him a quick kiss on the cheek!

With that, Catherine heads down the street toward the town square to watch. She finds a perfect viewing spot right near the tree and watches the marching bands and dance troupes lead the way in for Santa and Mrs. Holly Berry.

As Santa and Mrs. Holly Berry come into sight the choir leads the crowd in signing "We Wish You a Merry Christmas." She waves to Santa along with the rest of the crowd. After the float passes through town, the crowd disperses, and she walks over to the café near the town tree to wait for Blake. As soon as he finds her, he comes close and wraps her warmly in a hug.

"What did you think of the parade?" he asks.

"Santa's float was my favorite part," she says.

Catherine feels elated walking through the town square decorated for Christmas, with this new guy by her side. They pass a corner café with lights and garlands around the door.

"How about some hot chocolates to warm up?" she suggests.

"I'll grab us a table with a view of the town tree," he says.

As Catherine leaves the café, she sees a woman walking up to Blake and giving him a kiss on the lips, and put her hand in his, and he doesn't pull away. Catherine stands back near the doorway and watches as the woman wraps her arms around Blake's waist and rests her head on his shoulder. She recognizes the woman as Mrs. Holly Berry from her costume. She slowly walks back to Blake and Mrs. Holly Berry.

"Blakey sweetie, your float was genius! Simply delightful!" she hears Mrs. Holly Berry say.

"Ginger? You didn't tell me you were going to be Mrs. Holly Berry," Catherine says.

"I thought you knew? I am always Mrs. Holly Berry."

"What did I miss?" Catherine asks.

"Ginger, what are you doing here?" Blake asks.

"I thought you missed me!" Ginger teases.

"You two know each other?" Catherine asks.

"We have talked about this, Ginger," Blake says.

"I know, but you have been so busy lately!" Ginger whines.

Catherine sees Ginger rubbing his arm now.

"Nothing is different."

"I saw your ring at home and thought we might want to talk about things."

"His ring?" Catherine asks.

She can't believe what she is hearing and drops her hot chocolates and they splatter as they hit the pavement.

"You're married? To Mrs. Holly Berry Ginger?" Catherine questions.

"Are you trying to steal my man?" Ginger asks Catherine.

"Girls, don't fight. There's enough for everyone," Blake jokes.

"How could I have been so stupid? I trusted you!"

"No, it's not like that. You don't understand."

Blake touches Catherine's elbow, but she pushes him away.

"Catherine! You don't understand!" Blake says.

She pushes her way through the crowd, blinded by the tears. Racing to get home, the heel of her boot breaks.

"Damn it! Just my luck!"

Shivering from the cold and limping with her broken boot she begins to walk home in the dark. However, her anguish is interrupted by honking and headlights on the side of the road.

Blake stops the car next to her and rolls down the window. "Catherine, get in the car," he hollers.

She doesn't stop walking. "No, I am not riding home with you."

"Catherine, you'll freeze to death, it's four miles to your house and it's starting to snow."

"I don't care. Go away, Blake!"

"Please get in the car before something happens to you! I will get you home and you can be rid of me in ten minutes."

Catherine stops walking to consider her options and decides to get in the car. She shoves the papers piled on the seat out of the way to make room and climbs in his truck. The only noise between them is the crunch of the tires on the snowy road. Blake pulls into her driveway and puts the car in park. He turns on the cabin light and picks up the papers Catherine had shoved off the seat.

"Ginger came to town to give me these papers," Blake says.

Catherine looks over at him, but doesn't say a word, urging him to continue.

"They are divorce papers."

Catherine nods, opens the door, and climbs out of the truck. She starts to shut the truck door, but stops and looks up at Blake.

"I think this is all happening too fast. I don't even know you."

She watches Blake pull out of her driveway and then yanks open the door of her house and trips over Blake's toolbox in the mudroom. She picks it up and tosses it into the driveway and slams the door shut, locking the deadbolt. She walks into the great room and sees the drape cloths hanging around the room to minimize the dust from the work in the kitchen. She yanks at the tarp tearing it down, trying to put her house back the way it was. In her mind she's seething, *all the changes need to stop!* She pulls down the last tarp and collapses to her knees hugging it close to her chest.

Everywhere she looks everything is new and different and a mess. She can't see Aleksandra anywhere in this house. What is she doing here if she isn't here, too? She just wants to clean all this up and make it go back to the way it was before. She thought this work would make everything better, but it is just worse. All the signs of her life with Aleksandra are erased.

Trembling, she puts her head down feeling the cold of the hardwood floor on her face. She is struggling to get a breath. It feels like she's drowning and gasping for air. She remembers the prescription in her purse and crawls on her hands and knees to the mudroom to find her purse. It's buried under shoes in the bottom of the hall closet. Dumping everything to the floor, she struggles to twist off the child proof cap and all the pills spill out everywhere. She scoops two up and swallows them without water. As she sits amidst the mess waiting for the anti-anxiety medicine to kick in, she sees a flicker and reaches for her phone and without thinking dials Nelly.

"Hey sweetie!" Nelly says.

Catherine hears Nelly answer, but she is still gasping for breath and can't speak.

"What's going on? Are you ok?" Nelly asks.

"She's gone," Catherine gasps.

"Who's gone?" Nelly asks.

"Aleksandra, she's gone!" Catherine says.

"I know sweetie. She's been gone for over a year now."

"No! You don't understand, she was here and now she isn't."

"I know."

"I tried to fix it, but I made it worse," Catherine cries.

"What did you try to fix?"

"I just want it back the way it was. Now she's gone. I can't get her back."

"Shhh Shhh, it's ok."

"I'm so tired. I can't do this anymore. I'm all alone."

"You're not alone. You hear me. I'm coming right now. Don't move. I will be there in 2 hours."

Catherine drops the phone and wanders through the great room and down to the lake. She crawls into her Adirondack chair under the old oak tree at the edge of the water. With the reflection of the moon over the lake she can see the weathered spot on the tree from where the lightning struck years ago in a summer storm. She wonders what the tree felt when struck by lightning. She wonders if the bark will heal or bear the scar forever.

There was a time she had envisioned Aleksandra getting married in the Gazebo by this very tree. Her thoughts drift as she imagines what that day would have looked like with the tree in full bloom in the spring. Now it may never bloom again. She sits in the quiet with her thoughts and loneliness. All her tears have dried up and she feels empty. There's nothing left.

"Hey, I have been looking all over for you," Nelly calls out.

Catherine jumps at the sound of Nelly's voice.

"No bother, I found you now. What are you doing out here, it is freezing? Your hands, they are like ice!" Nelly says.

Nelly carefully wraps Catherine up in the blanket she brought down from the house and then settles into the chair next to her.

"The lake is pretty, all frozen like this," she says.

Catherine doesn't say anything. She doesn't even seem to hear her talking.

Nelly reaches over and holds Catherine's hand and gently strokes it.

"It's ok, we don't have to talk about it," Nelly says.

In the days that follow that blanket never leaves her shoulders and there is more silence than talk. For nearly a week, Nelly stays close, offering comfort despite the silence, knowing Catherine will open up and talk when she is ready. Catherine passes the days curled up on the couch. Nelly sits with her, makes her tea, and encourages her to eat, though she usually refuses.

Then it happens. Catherine wakes up, appreciating the

sun pouring in the windows of her bedroom and feeling hungry for the first time in days. Her heart is full of gratitude for Nelly, not just for the past days, but for the last year of her patient and loving care. Catherine showers, dresses, and tip toes down to the kitchen, letting Nelly sleep, so she can get started with breakfast.

"I made coffee!" Catherine announces cheerily when she sees Nelly coming down the stairs yawning, still in her pajamas.

Nelly, still groggy, picks up the mug taking a sip. Catherine's phone rings and she hits ignore on the call and sets it back down.

"I am also making some blueberry pancakes," Catherine says.

"I see someone is feeling better. Who was calling you this early?" Nelly asks.

"More coffee?" Catherine laughs at Nelly's grogginess.

Catherine's phone rings and she ignores the call again and switches the ringer off and sets it on the island face down.

"By the way, why haven't I seen Blake all week?"

"Trust me, we don't need him."

"So, it's him? Is that who's been calling you all week?"

"Like I said, I don't need him."

"What happened between you two?"

"I just misunderstood what was going on. I should have kept things strictly professional."

"It doesn't have to be like this."

"Like what?"

"You don't always have to go it alone."

"I don't always go it alone. I have you!"

"Listen to me. I know you want it to stop hurting and I wish I could give that to you, but you can't erase all the pain and memories just by selling her horse and putting a coat of paint on the walls. You can't run away from this."

Catherine doesn't answer and turns her attention to flipping the pancakes and warming the maple syrup.

"You have to admit he was right about the horse."

"Really? Now I have to hear it from you?"

"It seems to me that he really cares about you."

"I don't think that's true."

"Then why does he keep calling you? Just tell me you will think about talking to him."

"I'll think about it, but it is time you get back home to your family now. I'm sure they've missed you."

Catherine opens the door for Nelly to go and is surprised to find Blake in her driveway. Nelly wraps her in a hug good-bye and whispers, "just hear him out!"

Chapter 12

Catherine steps out onto the front porch and waves good-bye to Nelly as she pulls out of the driveway. She crosses her arms across her chest, partly because she is trying to keep herself warm, but mostly because she is annoyed at Blake appearing in her driveway.

"Blake! What are you doing here?" Catherine asks.

"I have a surprise for you," Blake says.

How could he possibly make up for the fact that he kept his marriage a secret from her? She thinks.

Then she watches as Blake lowers the tail gate to his truck and pulls out a 10' tall Fraser Fir Christmas tree.

"I thought your house needed a little Christmas spirit. A real tree is my favorite part of the season and you can't beat the fresh pine smell. We could set it up in your living room windows and hang some string lights and add some ornaments."

"I don't need a tree. I'm not celebrating Christmas," Catherine says.

"I've been calling you all week to apologize. You won't

take my calls or reply to my texts and I didn't know what to do," Blake says.

Catherine just stares at him without replying.

"Can we at least talk about the other night? Just hear me out."

Catherine agrees to hear him out and plops down on the sofa and waits for him to explain things.

"Ginger is my wife, but it is complicated. I guess I didn't mention it because I have felt divorced for years. I have been living up here for the last 8 years while she lived in the city. We each have our own lives and she came to town to get me to sign these divorce papers." Blake says, pulling out the divorce papers and showing them to Catherine.

Catherine thinks back on how Ginger had described her marriage, how it had been over before it started, and realizes that things are as Blake describes. However, she still doesn't understand why they stayed married for so long.

"Why didn't you just get divorced all those years ago?" Catherine asks.

"Her dad is a bigshot in the city and she was worried that a divorce would get splashed across the society pages and be an embarrassment. Apparently, she's met someone new and wants to move on now," Blake says.

Catherine thinks about Gingers larger than life personality compared to her. She has more emotional baggage than anyone would want to sign up for.

"I don't understand how you could be married to her and then be interested in me," Catherine says.

"I dunno," he says, waving a hand to the side as if trying to offer up the air as explanation. "Listen, I had spent years working hard to take care of Zach and Jennifer, and when I met Ginger, she was fresh and new, and… I felt like she was reminding me what it felt like to be alive, and all the fun I'd missed by having a family when I was so young."

"So why would you let that go?" Catherine asks.

"Believe me," he says. "I don't love her anymore. Soon after we got married she wanted to settle down. She wanted me to leave my business to work in her daddy's firm. I didn't recognize her as the carefree woman I married. I wanted to make her happy, so I moved to the city, but I felt suffocated and trapped. I missed the mountain air and the sun's reflection on the lake and watching the snow fall on the mountains in the winter."

"Why didn't you just ask her to come here?"

"It was too slow out here. She missed her girlfriends and the shops and restaurants and night life. We realized we were just too different. That's when I came out here and she stayed in the city."

"I don't even know why this matters. It's not like anything is going on with us."

"I guess I thought, maybe there was something between us," he says, tentatively stepping closer.

"I like the smell of real trees at Christmas, too," Catherine responds.

"So you will let me set it up?" Blake asks.

Catherine nods her head.

"I saw how happy you looked at the Holly Berry Festival singing along with the carolers. I thought you would be excited. I'm sorry."

Blake sits down next to Catherine and pulls her close to him. He wraps his arms around her to comfort her. She accepts his warmth and even puts her head on his shoulder and quietly cries.

"I know it won't be the same, but I am here now and you don't have to do this alone. The renovations will be done by Christmas and it will look so much more festive with a tree. Will you let me put the tree up for you?"

"I think the Christmas decorations are in the attic."

They head up to the attic and pull the string and the light bulb illuminates. Catherine moves some boxes around in the dark corner and takes the lid off checking the contents.

"Over here, I found them!"

Blake carries the boxes down to the living room, where the tree is in the stand. He strings the lights on, while Catherine watches and thinks back on her Christmases with Aleksandra. Their tradition was to make hot cocoa with extra marshmallows and turn on Christmas carols before they started the decorating. After the lights and ornaments went on, they would string popcorn and cranberries as a garland for the tree and to hang on the deck for the birds. When the tree was finished they would start a fire and turn off all the lights except for the tree, and snuggle under blankets and watch Christmas movies with the fire and Christmas tree lights twinkling in the background.

"We are ready for the ornaments now!"

Catherine opens up the box of ornaments and pulls out one that was handmade. On the back Aleksandra had scrawled her name and age: five. Her teacher had painted her hand and turned it into a Santa Clause. The fingers were his beard, the palm of the hand was his face and then a red felt hat with a white pom-pom was glued on top. She carefully and tenderly places it on the front of the tree. The ornaments were collected from their life together. From the glass blown crab they bought on a beach trip, the Santa Statue of Liberty from their visit to New York City,

and the clothes pin Rudolph made in preschool, each orna-
ment tells a moment in their life together.

"There, I think that does it."

They step back to admire the tree. He puts a fresh log
on the fire and they curl up on the couch and watch "It's a
Wonderful Life".

"I don't want you to spend this Christmas alone. Tell
me you will come to Christmas with my family,"
Blake says.

He puts his hand gently on her shoulder, reassuring
her. "When I saw your panic over the boots and with her
horse, I knew you were going through something very
hard, but I didn't know what, but Nelly told me everything
that happened."

Catherine looks out over the frozen lake, enjoying the cozy
morning on the couch. Her mind replays the moments
from the night before with Blake, until the phone interrupts her reverie.

"Jim, how have you been?" Catherine asks.

"I know it's early, I hope I didn't wake you," Jim says.

"No, you're fine," Catherine says.

"Good, good! And I certainly hope you are better than
the last time we spoke," Jim says.

"Yes, I am doing much better. I think the fresh air and
rest have been good for me."

"I am glad to hear that because I need you back,"
Jim says.

"What do you mean, you need me back?"

"Haven't you been reading your emails? I am being
bought out!"

"Yes, of course… I will call my team straight away and
make sure they walk you through every step of the deal."

"No, that isn't going to work. I have worked my entire career for this deal and I need YOU here to make sure everything goes smoothly."

"You know I have a great team, and they care about you and your business."

"These youngsters insist they can modernize the technology and reach one billion dollars in sales this year. I think they are rushing things."

"Let me check in with my team, I'm confident, Anna can handle this."

"No one knows my business like you do! I have been waiting over 20 years for a deal like this. This is a critical time for me, so I expect to see you at my office on Monday at 9 AM."

Catherine pauses on the phone and picks up Blake's scarf from the back of the couch, wrapping it around herself and rubbing the ends of the cashmere between her fingers. She feels so safe here with Blake, but the house is empty without Aleksandra. She thought she knew what she wanted. She was just coming here to fix the house and sell it, but now it's complicated. Blake is the first guy she's been interested in for a long time.

"Catherine, are you there? I need an answer."

"Ok, Jim, I understand. You can count on me. I'll see you at the office Monday morning and we'll work through all the details."

Chapter 13

On Sunday afternoon, Blake parks the truck in front of his mom and dad's house. The pine trees surrounding the house are coated in a fresh blanket of snow. Smoke is billowing out of the chimney and there is frost on the windows. As soon as Catherine steps in the front door, she's greeted by the smell of the turkey cooking and the sounds of holiday cheer from Blake's family. It feels like Christmas.

A woman pulls Catherine into a warm hug, rocking her from side to side, which Catherine awkwardly accepts.

"I'm Blake's sister, Kelly," the woman shares. "I'm so excited to meet you. Blake has told me so many wonderful things about you."

Catherine looks over to Blake and back at his sister, Kelly. Then scanning the room, she takes in the kids running through the house and the buzz of the adults talking and laughing.

"I haven't been to a holiday quite like this before," Catherine says.

"Welcome to the family fun! I will be your tour guide," Kelly bosses, taking Catherine's hand and leading her into the kitchen. "Blake, take Catherine's coat. You know where Mom likes them."

The kitchen is warm from cooking and there she meets Blake's mom who is humming Christmas carols while stirring something on the stove.

"You have to try Mom's famous Christmas punch," Kelly says, pouring Catherine a mug.

With her punch in hand, they step into the living room where most of the family is gathered. There is a fire crackling in the fireplace and a brightly lit colorfully decorated tree in the far corner.

Blake puts his arm around Catherine. "Let me introduce you to my family."

"Luke and Chris and Michael, this is my girlfriend Catherine. Catherine, these are my crazy brothers," Blake teases.

Catherine blushes and shakes their hands as one of the little boys in the room runs over and hugs the brother she thinks is named Luke.

"Can we open presents now, Daddy?" the boy whines.

"This is my youngest, Jake. Jake, did you say hi to Uncle Blake's friend Catherine?" Luke asks.

"You may remember Jake from the hockey game, where I scored the winning goal," Blake says as he messes up the boy's hair playfully.

"Who wants to open presents?" Blake's mom asks cheerfully.

"Taking a break from the cooking?" Blake asks, giving his mom a warm hug.

Catherine remembers how she loved to cook the big holiday dinner and make the perfect gravy and creamiest mashed potatoes. Just when everything was about perfect, she would take a break and sip her holiday wassail and watch Aleksandra open her presents from her grandparents. Catherine feels herself getting choked up at the memory, but hides her expression behind her punch glass, as she anxiously watches the kids opening gifts.

"What are you waiting for? Rip them open," Blake's dad teases and the kids start shouting with excitement as they open their presents. She watches Jake hurriedly ripping the wrapping paper off a package and flinging it around the room. He stands up hugging his new toy and dancing in celebration. She finds a spot to sit down on the couch watching and trying to soak in their joyous energy.

"Show me what you got," she asks the little boy. "Wow that looks so fun! Can you show me how it works?"

She is hoping no one can hear the sadness in her voice as she strains to hide how her heart is breaking in a million pieces by wearing a big smile and playing with the kids. As Jake shows her his new toy, she takes a deep breath trying to compose herself.

It isn't fair for my sadness to ruin their day, I don't want to be that person that brings the mood of the party down, she thinks.

She swallows hard holding back tears and pastes on her smile, continuing to watch the kids play, and even posing for selfies with them. Jake hugs her tight before running back to play with the other kids. She fears she can't hide the tears any longer and excuses herself.

Catherine locks the bathroom door behind her. She picks up the tissue box on the vanity but finds it empty. Opening the door of the linen closet, a stack of towels falls which knocks down the bottles of shampoo and cleaners stored on the shelf below. She hopes no one hears the loud crash on the tile floor. Kneeling down to pick everything, she collapses and cries. *What am I doing here? What was I thinking? I can barely get through a normal day, what was I thinking coming to a big joyous family holiday! I can't just replace what I had with his family.*

"Sweetheart, dinner's ready," Blake says, gently knocking on the door.

"I will be down in just a minute," she says, reaching into the mess surrounding her and grabbing a box of tissues.

She stands up, pulls out a tissue, and leans back against the vanity, tilting her head back and dabbing at the tears flowing down her cheeks. She closes her eyes, trying to quiet the emotions welling up inside her, but she can't hold it back anymore. They're like a runaway train that can't be stopped. Turning to look in the mirror she sees her eyes are red and her cheeks stained with the tears that escaped.

How am I staring at myself crying in the bathroom mirror again? She thinks. *I just want to be able to enjoy the excitement of Christmas morning without all the pain and sadness. Will I ever have that again?* She wonders.

Exhaling loudly, she shakes her arms and legs trying to release all that she's feeling. She gives herself a pep talk, reminding herself how lucky she is to be surrounded by so many loving people. She wipes off her tears one final time and practices her fake smile in the mirror. Then checks her makeup one last time before opening the bathroom door to rejoin the party.

Blake is waiting for her in the hallway as she leaves the bathroom. He puts his arm around her, pulling her in for a gentle squeeze and plants a kiss on her cheek. "Everyone is sitting down for dinner," Blake says, escorting her into the dining room.

As they enter together, Catherine notices how much attention was given to setting up the room for their dinner. Blake's mom has set the main table with a red tablecloth and festive napkins with a red and green pattern of holly leaves and berries. There are candles in a wreath in the center of the table. The turkey is golden brown, sitting on a platter at the head of the table, waiting to be carved. A handmade gingerbread house is the centerpiece of the kids table, with a plastic Santa Claus table cloth.

Everyone looks for their place card and finds their chairs when Blake's dad taps his glass to call attention for the dinner blessing. A hush falls over the room while he shares how grateful he is to have everyone together on this holiday. He then signals the start of dinner by carving the turkey. Blake reaches over and gives her hand a tender squeeze and smiles at her, and she feels herself relax and join in the laughter at the table.

"How is your renovation project going, Blake?" Kelly asks.

"It's wonderful. The house looks amazing and the best part is that it was done ahead of schedule. You love the changes right, honey?" Blake asks.

He puts his arm around Catherine pulling her into a side hug and smiling broadly with pride over his work on her house.

"He has really made it so beautiful," Catherine says.

"I told you that you would fall in love with my work and never be able to leave it," Blake teases.

"I think this calls for a toast," Blake's brother announces.

Blake's mom pulls out the champagne and pours everyone a glass.

Catherine watches how supportive they are of each other and wonders if she ever had an experience of family and acceptance like this. Blake hands her a glass of champagne and stands up to announce his toast.

"To new beginnings," Blake says, looking directly at Catherine.

"To new beginnings," everyone at the table echoes.

"I think you made the right decision in choosing to stay," Blake's sister says.

Blake leans over and kisses Catherine gently on the cheek, his smile stretching from ear to ear.

Catherine looks at Blake, "Jim called last night. He has a big deal on the table and needs me back at the office," she blurts out.

Blake sits up straighter. "You're going back?" he asks.

Catherine just nods her head.

"When?"

"I have to drive back tonight."

"That sounds like a wonderful opportunity, honey," Blake's mom says.

Blake's sister stands to clear dishes from the table, squeezing Blake's shoulder as she passes by.

"Congratulations," Blake's sister adds.

Catherine climbs into the cab of Blake's truck. He is wearing sadness like a coat as he starts the truck in silence. As they drive, Catherine looks out the window at the snowy roofs trimmed in Christmas lights. She's lost in her thoughts. Blake pulls into her driveway and puts the truck in park and takes the key out. He reaches for her hands as the cabin lights turn on.

"I wanted to tell you alone. I'm sorry, I didn't mean to ruin the holiday."

"Why do you want to go?" Blake asks.

"This is my life! I have spent over twenty years building my business and I can't just walk away from it."

"I'm not asking you to walk away from it."

"This deal is huge for Jim's company and I want to be there for him."

"And what about us?"

"What I came to do here is done, and now I have to get back home. I have to get back to my real life."

"Are you saying what we have isn't real?"

She stares at him icily trying to cover the sadness and hold back the tears. *Why doesn't he understand that I can't abandon Aleksandra?*

"You always knew my life is back home and I need to get back to it now," Catherine says.

"Your life could be here. Why won't you let me in?" Blake asks.

"I just want one day where I don't have to cry. Is that too much to want? I don't think I can be with you until then," Catherine says.

"Don't you know your heart is safe with me?" Blake asks, reaching for her hand.

"I have to get packed and drive home tonight, so I can make it to my meeting tomorrow," Catherine says.

She can see in his eyes that he loves her, but it's just too much for her. She has tried to move on, but can't. Now she fears she can't let go and will wake up and realize she could have had the love story of her dreams, but let it slip away. What if he is right? What if being here would be right for her?

Chapter 14

Hours later, she pulls into her garage back in the city. She opens the door to the mudroom and somehow it is colder inside than it is outside. She fumbles around in the darkness to find the light switch and flicks it on. Damnit! The bulb is burned out, and she trips over the coat tree dropping her purse and phone. Tracing her hands along the wall, she reaches for the flashlight in the cabinet. She finds her way to the living room but the lights there don't go on either. Finally, she heads to the electric panel to flip on the breaker. With lights working again, she can head back upstairs to turn the heat back on.

Still cold, she bundles up, grabs extra blankets, and crawls into bed to rest for her meeting early the next morning.

The next thing she remembers, a loud beeping sound jolts her awake. She looks around confused until she sees the clock, 4 AM, and remembers she needs to prepare for her meeting with Jim. She drags herself down to the kitchen and brews a strong pot of coffee and boots up her computer. Huge mug of coffee in hand, she opens her email and digs into the notes that Jim's team sent over. After three hours she has detailed notes for each discussion point. She stretches her back, tired from hunching over her computer, and heads to her closet to get ready.

The days of the jeans and sweaters are over and it's time to pull out her Navy Blue suit and heels. She picks out a freshly cleaned pair of suit pants and holds them up for inspection.

Size 2? Whose pants are these? My arm won't even fit into these, she thinks, not remembering how tiny she was. She checks through all the other pants and suit skirts and they are all just as tiny. She tries to squeeze into them but can't pull them up over her thighs, much less get them zipped for the meeting.

What am I going to wear? Stores aren't open at this hour! Panicking, she spots the leggings she just bought and slides them on. She grabs the longest black blazer she can find and races to her meeting.

She walks confidently into Jim's office. "Hi Julie, is Jim ready?"

While walking down the hallway to Jim's office she fidgets, feeling overexposed, awkwardly tugging at the hem of her jacket trying to pull it down over her butt.

Jim stands to greet them as they enter his office. "Catherine, I am so glad you are here. They are circling this place like a pack of wolves."

Walking down the hallway to the conference room, Jim pauses and cocks his head sideways, taking her in, and says, "is this part of your plan to put yourself back out there, or is this look you are wearing hipster bait for our meeting?"

"Just don't ask!" And they walk into the conference room.

They enter the conference room together and confront four young men all wearing skinny black suit pants, blue button up shirts and matching eye frames. She decides she has to concur with Jim's hipster assessment.

"Looks like we are all here now, so let's start with point one on our agenda," the lead hipster declares.

"Let's slow down and take a minute to get to know one another," Jim interrupts.

"This is Catherine. She has been my CPA for over 20 years now. I knew she was the best the minute I met her and had to have her on my team. She wouldn't join me as CFO, so she has been my CPA since day one. She knows everything about this business."

"Great to meet you, I'm Zane, now let's get started with point one on our agenda," the lead hipster says again.

Catherine feels her phone buzz and pulls it from her bag and sees a text from Blake. "Just signed the divorce papers."

"Good for you," Catherine texts coldly.

"Things aren't the same here without you." Catherine swipes the notification off and closes her phone without replying.

"Catherine, Zane is asking about the projected dip in 4th quarter revenue," Jim repeats, annoyed that she wasn't paying attention to the discussion. She realizes she zoned out. On top of missing the question, she doesn't know which one of the hipsters Jim is referring to.

She looks in the direction of their leader. "Zane," and begins.

"I am Zach."

"Good to know." Jim glares at her flippant response.

She continues, "my apologies, with reference to revenue, it is important to note that most of Vertus Technologies' customers are government agencies, which have a fiscal year end of September 30th. They accelerate payments to Vertus during this time to use up any

remaining portion of their budget, which causes a dip in
4th quarter revenue. However, if you look at the year over
year, you will see revenue increased by 5.7% in the current
year, which is above market standards."

"For a minute I was worried you were losing your
touch, but you didn't miss a step," Jim says to her as he
walks her out.

"That's why I am the best and you love me!" Catherine
laughs nervously, unsure of how she feels about being
back, and offers a weak wave as she heads out the door.

Catherine climbs in her car and her phone rings and she
picks it up.

"Oh, hi Richard!"

"Catherine, I'm so glad I caught you. I wanted to let
you know I have an offer on your place!"

"An offer?"

"Yes, full price, cash offer!"

"Full price?"

"Yes, isn't that wonderful? They want a quick close.
How does New Year's Eve sound?"

"That's less than a week away."

"I know, I told you I would sell it by New Year's. I am
going to email the contract over to you. I need it signed
today."

"Ok. Thanks, Richard."

"Congratulations!"

As soon as she hangs up from Richard, Catherine hears
her phone ringing again. She sits in her car holding her
ringing phone, thinking about whether or not to answer
Nelly's call. She has so much to share with the news from

Richard and the meeting with Jim, but Nelly wouldn't understand. *She won't get how I feel.* On the fourth ring she finally accepts the call and agrees to meet her and the kids at the playground.

Catherine parks her car at the playground and watches Nelly's two older kids, Olivia and Cooper, climb up the ladder of the sliding board and slide down. Aleksandra's favorite was always the tire swing in circles, faster and faster. Just watching the tire swing made Catherine feel motion sick. Catherine sees Nelly pushing her youngest, Tyler, in the stroller and climbs out of the car to join her.

Nelly greets Catherine with a hug.

"They have all gotten so big," Catherine says, looking at Tyler sitting in the stroller.

"Cooper, don't eat the mulch," Nelly shouts at him. "He is four now, I thought we were done with that stage where they put everything in their mouth."

"I'm afraid I've missed so much,"

"Let's sit down on the bench and you can tell me how your meeting with Jim went," Nelly says.

Catherine feels hesitant to share. Nelly wouldn't understand. She had given up her career dreams for her family. Catherine sits on the bench, lost in her thoughts.

"What are you not telling me?" Nelly prods her.

Catherine is watching Olivia cross the monkey bars and Cooper still playing with the mulch.

"I got an offer on the house. They want to close on New Year's Eve," Catherine says.

"That's only a few days away!" Nelly says, surprised.

"The meeting with Jim went great. To be honest, it felt amazing to be back. You should have seen me set those hipsters straight and close the deal for Jim. Now he can be sure they won't be dismantling his business anytime soon," Catherine beams proudly.

"Wow, I haven't seen this side of you in so long," Nelly says. "But something's different. What's up?"

"I don't know, it is all just happening so fast now," Catherine says.

"You mean it is all coming together again," Nelly says.

"Maybe. I should be happy, but I just feel confused. Something feels off. I feel like I don't fit anywhere now."

"It was a hard year and now you've been away a while. You probably just need some time to adjust back into the routine," Nelly says.

"I was always so happy here, but now it just feels empty," Catherine says.

"Is it Blake?"

Catherine just blushes, thinking about the time she has spent with Blake.

"Sometimes you have to make hard choices about what's most important to you." Nelly says.

"I already did that in my life and then when I lost Aleksandra - I felt alone."

"I know, nothing has gone as planned. But now things are changing. Life is compromises," Nelly says.

"What if I don't want to compromise anymore? I want to have it all, I am going to have it all. I am going to be a superstar at work and have love and a family! Just watch!"

"Keep dreaming!" Nelly laughs.

Catherine picks up her phone from her purse and sees an incoming call from her real estate agent.

"Excuse me, but I have to take this," Catherine says.

"We have a problem and I need you to get back here right away," Richards says.

"What happened?"

"A pipe froze and there's quite a bit of damage," Richard responds.

. . .

"Call Blake, he'll know what to do," Nelly says.

"I don't think he's happy that I am planning to leave, and I doubt he'll want to help me," Catherine says.

"He cares about you and he won't let you down, just call him."

"I better get going and drive back to the lake to make sure everything is fixed before the buyers back out," Catherine says. She pulls Nelly close, as if to say thank you.

"Call him!" Nelly teases.

"Why are you such a good friend to me?" she asks, giving Nelly a kiss goodbye on the cheek.

Chapter 15

Catherine opens the door to the lake house and makes her way to the basement. As she walks through the house she takes in all the changes. After having been away for a few days she sees them with fresh eyes and can't believe the transformation her house has undergone.

It had looked tired and sad when Blake started and now it feels like a fresh and welcoming home. She heads down the stairs and as she approaches the storage room, her feet splash through the water that is pooling in the basement. She stops and stares into the water, unsure of what to do.

I've always known what I wanted, but now I don't know anymore, Catherine thinks. She's startled to hear noise behind her and swirls around to see Blake.

"Sorry, I didn't realize you were back, so I let myself in," he says.

"Richard called me as soon as it happened," Catherine says.

"You're lucky he knew where the main water shut-off

valve is and stopped the flow of water quickly, so there isn't too much damage," Blake says.

Catherine just looks around at the small lake forming in her storage room, feeling overwhelmed.

"Don't worry, it's not as bad as it seems. I will replace the broken pipe and use a wet vac to get the water out of here and then I will replace the drywall and paint," Blake says.

"Ok," she says and blushes, wondering how he is so patient with her.

"You will be as good as new in about 48 hours. I know you're worried about fixing it before the new owners arrive," Blake says, walking back upstairs.

They stand in the storage room in an awkward silence for what feels like an eternity, before Blake asks, "how did things go at your meeting?"

"At first, I felt a little rusty, but it turns out I haven't lost my edge," Catherine says.

"I am happy for you. Wait, were you wearing those pants the whole time?" Blake asks.

"It was the only thing in my closet that fit!" she says, laughing comfortably and hitting him in the arm.

"So I guess that's it. You're really going back?" Blake asks.

"When I'm there, I feel like I have a purpose. I'm really good at what I do. If I give that up, what is left of me?"

"What have you been doing out here all these months?"

"Did you know that I used to draw when I was younger? I'm sure it is hard to imagine knowing me now, but I was good at it and I liked it."

"Why didn't you pursue it?"

"I thought about it, but wasn't willing to risk it. If I kept it a secret for myself I could just enjoy it. If I shared it with the world then I had to be vulnerable and open myself up to the criticism or rejection. I poured my heart and soul into my work, what if I shared it and they said it wasn't good enough? Do you know what that feels like?"

"I think I do, but what if they loved it and wanted to keep it forever?"

"I don't know if I am willing to find out," Catherine says.

"I understand, but I can't be around you while you figure this out," Blake says.

Catherine's eyes flash with hurt and sadness. "That's probably best, because this just shows that you don't get me at all," Catherine says, wondering how he could abandon her now.

"Just for the record, this is not me leaving you. You're shutting me out," Blake says.

"I don't understand. Why are you doing this?" Catherine asks.

"It was good to see you again, Catherine," Blake says.

He picks up his toolbox and heads out to his truck.

"You too," Catherine says as she tenderly shuts the door behind him.

"I'll miss you," Catherine whispers to herself after she closes the door. Her hand rests on the door handle, her heart aching and feeling so alone again.

Catherine pulls open all the curtains and blinds, letting in the natural sunlight. From the looks of it you'd think it was early spring rather than late December. As she looks out the window, she notices that a light dusting of snow fell overnight, leaving a fresh white coating on the deck and the pine trees outlining the yard. She steps outside to make sure the walkway is clear and hears the car doors slamming, which means the real estate agent and buyers have arrived for their final walk through.

She opens up the front door and goes down the walkway to welcome them to their almost home. However, something catches her eye on the path. She bends down and wipes the snow off the patch of walkway and she sees Aleksandra's tiny handprints. She gasps and puts her hands down on top of them to feel how tiny she was.

She remembers that afternoon, was Aleksandra four or five that summer? It's hard to remember now, but she can picture it as clearly as if it were yesterday. They had been playing with their puppy, Tulip, in the yard down by the dock while a crew worked to replace their old gravel path into a concrete walkway. It was late in the day when the foreman came to let Catherine know that the driveway was poured and smoothed, so they were ready to head out. He wanted her to approve it before the crew left for the day. As he showed her his work, he reminded her that the concrete would firm in a few hours and be set within 24 hours. While she was distracted finalizing, Aleksandra had wondered off to the edge and sunk her hands deep into the still wet concrete leaving her tiny handprints.

Catherine recalls how she heard Aleksandra laughing and the dog barking when she turned to see her with her hands smooshed into the concrete. She remembers how furious she was and how she berated her about the thousands of dollars she just spent to have the perfect sidewalk installed, and in two minutes Aleksandra had destroyed it. As she remembers how angry she was and how Aleksandra had just giggled about it, tears come to her eyes.

In this moment her heart swells with love for her daughter. She spent over a year avoiding this place in order to avoid the pain of losing Aleksandra, and in this brief moment her heart nearly explodes with joy as she feels at home. She feels like Aleksandra has called her there to remind her that this is their true home. The place of a thousand happy memories and laughs. The place that holds all their joy and love. The place of her spirit. She knows she needs to stop running away and instead choose to embrace the love they shared. The way to keep her alive forever is to embrace her spirit. To remember all they shared. The only way to live is through her love.

Catherine whispers a soft thank you to Aleksandra for calling her back to where she needs to be. Suddenly she remembers that the agent and buyers are waiting on her. She realizes that someone is speaking to her and she hasn't been listening. She hastily wipes the tears from her eyes with the cuff of her sweater and stands to greet them, apologizing for being distracted. She is overwhelmed by the excited buyers who don't seem to notice she had been crying, and their agent asking if it's ok to go inside and take a look around.

"No!" Catherine says.

They look at her confused.

"We thought our appointment was at 9 AM?" the agent asks.

Catherine sniffles, and nods her head, saying, "yes, the time is right, but I can't do this. This is my home and I need to stay here."

The buyers look bewildered and argue. "The truck is going to be here in a few hours. What are we supposed to do?" The husband is angry and shouting, "We have a contract!"

"I know. I'm sorry, but I just can't," Catherine says as she runs to the house.

She rushes into the house and stands there, frozen for a moment, before she starts frantically pacing back and forth in the living room, panicking about what she just did. *Now what? I have a home and a business and a life. What did I just do? Blake? Oh my goodness, I have to tell Blake.*

Catherine picks up Blake's scarf from the back of the couch. Again, looking out the living room window onto the lake, she remembers their afternoon ice skating.

When was the last time I let myself have fun like that? She thinks. *When was the last time I felt so safe with someone that I could let them in?*

She knows she needs to talk to him, but how? Picking up her phone, she texts Blake.

"I have your scarf and I thought you might want it back," Catherine texts.

"I'm at the ice rink watching my nephew play hockey," Blake replies.

Re-reading the text a few times, she is unsure of how to reply. *I have never done this before and I have already lost so much,* she thinks.

"I'm sorry, I kept you at a distance for so long," she writes.

"I'm sorry, it's just not a good time right now," Blake replies.

"There's something I need to tell you. Are you free to talk later?" Catherine asks.

"I'll be home in a few hours, come by then."

Catherine puts the phone down and walks through the yard to visit the horses. Tinka is playing in the outdoor ring and trots over to the fence where Catherine is approaching. Petting her nose, she nuzzles into Tinka's fuzzy winter coat. As Catherine scratches her neck, a light snow begins to fall, the fat white flakes dotting Tinka's dark fur.

"Well Tinka, I'm staying. I'm not going to leave you," Catherine says.

Catherine picks a soft brush out of the grooming bucket hanging on the fence post and brushes Tinka's fur and talks to her as she works.

"You were always a good listener when Aleksandra needed you. Maybe you can do that for me, too?" Catherine asks. "I think I may have messed this up. What if I have waited too long?"

She returns the brush to the bucket and heads in the barn, returning with a clean blanket and secures it on Tinka.

"Here, this will keep you warm."

She tenderly pats Tinka's neck and gives her a kiss.

"I guess I will never be ready, so here goes nothing. Wish me luck, girl."

Driving up to Blake's cabin, her heart races and her stomach flips. With the car in park she takes a breath and thinks, *you can do this,* and practices what she wants to say to Blake.

Hearing a tap on the window, she turns to see Blake motioning for her to roll down the window.

"Can I get in on the conversation?" Blake asks.

She feels the heat rise to her face and turn a deep shade of red.

"How long have you been standing there?" she asks.

"Long enough," Blake teases.

He opens the door and offers her a hand as she climbs out of the car. When they reach the front porch, Mason and Annie hop up from their naps and race through the yard before greeting her with wagging tails. Catherine smiles and hands him his scarf.

"You left your scarf when we went ice skating," Catherine says.

"That's what you needed to talk to me about?" Blake asks.

"You're not making this easy on me."

"It's not easy for anyone."

"I wanted to tell you that I see it now. My future is here."

"What do you mean?" Blake asks.

"I didn't sell the house. I'm staying."

Blake shifts his weight from one foot to the other.

"And?"

"And, I'd like that future to include you," Catherine says.

Blake smiles. "I just wanted to hear you say it."

Catherine lets out a breath she didn't realize she had been holding in.

"I think, I love you," Catherine says.

"I know, I love you."

Catherine feels the tears starting again, but this time she cries with joy as Blake scoops her into his arms and swings her around. She laughs and he holds her tight.

"I love you, Blake," she whispers.

Blake sets her down and gently runs his fingers through her hair and pulls her in for a kiss.

THE END!

A Note From Katie

Thank you for reading *A New Beginning*. I trust that you enjoyed reading it as much as I enjoyed writing it for you.

Word of mouth helps me connect with new readers. If you enjoyed the story, please invite your family and friends to read it too. If you prefer, you can leave me a review! Even just a few words help other readers find the story.

I would love to connect with you, my reader, to hear what you thought about the book, or to just say hi. You can contact me through any of my social media links below.

Catherine and Blake will be back soon in Book 2 of Lakeside Hideaway series.

XO,
Katie

About the Author

Katie loves finding beauty and romance in every day, whether it is the first snow in the winter, the changing leaves of autumn, pink sunsets, or summers by the lake with her family. Katie Mongelli is a CPA and financial coach and after decades of reading love stories and romance novels she realized that writing romance is her favorite passion and created The Lakeside Hideaway Series.

If you want to know when Katie's next book will come out, please visit her at www.KatieMongelli.com.

 instagram.com/Katie.Mongelli

Acknowledgments

I am grateful for all the support I received during the process of writing this book. Thank you Emily Maher, I am so appreciative for your generous friendship, love, and support during this project. Thank you Marion Metz, you made the final editing process so easy. Alexis, thank you for believing in me and cheering me on every step of the way! My love, thank you for your unending love and encouragement. To all of my friends and family who have supported me and believed in me, thank you!